The following is a work of fiction, etc., etc....

Other works by Lucas D. James

I Am Simon Black
A Quiet Fury
I Never Saw the Spiders
Don't Call Me Lucky

"I am ninety-three percent the person I present in my poems...

"...the other seven percent is where art improves upon life."
~ Charles Bukowski

lucasdjames23@gmail.com

SHE CALLED ME THE DEVIL

Lucas D. James

PART ONE:
INTOXICATED BLOOD

Chapter 1

"That man is the devil," the old woman said to Kayla as she gestured toward me, standing on the other side of the back patio at the Hole in the Ground tavern laughing with a cigarette in one hand and a drink in the other, dressed in black with blue jeans. Kayla didn't tell me this story until months after it happened.

"What?" Kayla asked, caught off guard.

"You see that young man standing over there?" the old woman drunkenly pointed at me.

Kayla looked down my direction as my head turned toward her with a mischievous grin and a bit of curiosity before turning my attention back to my friends. "Yeah," Kayla replied. "What about him?"

The drunk old woman put her face close to Kayla's and said to her in badly slurred speech, "That man is the *devil*. You look in his eyes, there's blackness behind the blue, where the soul should be. Stay away from that one."

Kayla gave the old woman a baffled look. "Um… thanks, I guess." She listened to the old woman. She kept her distance from me for almost the entire night. She'd catch my eye every now and then, draped in a form fitting black dress with dark hair to match. She was one of the most beautiful women I had ever seen in my life. Classy. Sophisticated. Better than the average tumbleweed and shambling shitshow that normally stumbled through the place. She was too good for me. But I would catch her looking my way from time to time.

We all enjoyed the revelry and merriment of Friday night intoxication. All laughter and good times. Eventually, though, enough is enough and you just need a moment of peace and fucking quiet. Searching for some of that, I stepped out front and down the steps, taking up a little spot by the bar's front porch to smoke a cigarette in solitude, drunk past all point of caring. A couple people walked outside – a girl I had known from high school ten years ago and her new boyfriend.

"Hey, Stacey," I said nonchalantly.

"Oh hey," came her reply as she walked down the steps onto the sidewalk. Kayla stepped out the door just a moment later. Stacey's boyfriend looked down over the rail at me, smoking his own cigarette.

"You know her?" he asked, nodding toward his girlfriend.

"She used to ride my bus," I replied. Maybe could have picked my words more carefully because he seemed to think it was a euphemism.

"I swear to god, I'm so fucking tired of people hitting on my girl," the man said as he glared down at me over the rail.

My shoulders shrugged. "Shit happens, I guess. Don't let it fuck with you."

He descended the steps and stood in front of me. "I swear I'm gonna beat the fuck out of the next guy who does it."

Kayla made her way half way down the stairs, sat on the cold brick and pulled out a cigarette, coyly watching the interchange play out.

I replied, "Sounds like you've got some aggression in you, man. You should find an outlet." I reached my free hand out toward him. "Grip shake?" I asked. A grip shake is what I call it when two men grab each other's hands and see who can crush through the other person's grip first. Imagine the world's most aggressive handshake. It's stupid, but it's a good way to size somebody up.

He grabbed my hand in his and immediately began trying to break it. I'm not the world's biggest guy by any stretch of the fucking imagination, but years of moving kegs had given me some decent forearm strength. I had it where it counted. My hand gripped back against his.

To me it was just a stupid little game. I thought I was doing him a favor by letting him vent. Guy had a solid four or five inches on me and outweighed me by a couple dozen pounds, apparently he thought he would break my hand in a couple seconds. He got mad when that didn't happen.

"Come on," I joked, "that the best you got?" His face quickly showed more anger than anything else.

"You got a fucking problem?" he asked in a threatening tone. He began to close the short distance between us, his hand still trying to break mine.

"You've gotta have more in you than that," I replied laughing. Kayla watched with sideways glances, not wanting to get involved but not wanting to miss what was happening.

"You tryin' to fucking go?" the man asked me. He walked into me, our hands still firmly locked in place, his cigarette dangling in his mouth, and backed me into the wall. I couldn't contain my laughter. This fucking guy, so pissed and so fragile in his own ego that he was ready to go to blows over a goddamn handshake and a stranger saying hi to his girlfriend. "Something fucking funny?" he asked me.

"Yeah," I laughed in his face. "All of this. You're fucking hilarious." A few people had gathered around behind him, probably wanting to see a fight break out. "This is a fucking joke." He got so close to me his cigarette touched my cheek, leaving a nice little circular burn mark on my face. Then I laughed some more.

"I could fucking break you," he warned.

"I'd like to see you try." A grin stretched out across my face.

At that moment, one of my friends, Clyde the bouncer, came up behind him and pulled him off. His elbows flew back as he knocked my friend to the ground. Clyde could take care of himself, though. He was a little shorter than me but made of solid muscle. He got back up and hoisted the man by his shirt and tossed him into the street.

"Knock it the fuck off and get out of here," he commanded. "You're done for the night."

"Fuck this place," the man said defiantly, then spat effetely into the ground. Stacey looked embarrassed for him.

As they walked off, I shouted, "Bye Stacey!" and laughed to myself. Clyde shook his head and scoffed.

"You alright, bud?" he asked.

"Yeah, thanks."

He amicably slapped my shoulder then walked back inside. It was just me and Kayla sitting out there in silence. Finally, after a minute, she spoke.

"There's a cigarette burn on your face."

My finger touched my cheek, then I shrugged. "Call it a beauty mark. Way I see it, I need a few more scars anyway."

She let out a sort of confused laugh, unsure how to take my response. "That kind of thing happen a lot here?"

"Every other god damn night. My dad owns the place. I just work here."

"I guess I'll have to start coming here more often."

I looked at her. She was eyeing me up, trying to figure out what to make of me. "Yeah, you should." She slid down over to the other side of the steps, the side closer to me. "I'm Weston Ryder," I said, holding my hand out between the baluster slats to shake hers. "I usually just go by West."

She took it after a moment. "Kayla, Kayla Sparks."

We smiled at each other. "Pleasure." Neither of us knew it that night but we would go on to have a passionate, tumultuous relationship of heartbreak and disaster.

Two and a half years after we met, she went missing.

Chapter 2

My phone rang for the hundredth time as I laid in bed, hungover and sore. Izzy laid in bed next to me, neither of us making any real effort to get up despite the fact that it was nearly four in the afternoon on a Saturday. I let my phone go to voicemail, rolled over and wrapped my arm around the girl next to me. She was thin with strawberry blonde hair and a body that hit all of my weak spots. My phone rang again.

"Jesus Christ, West," she said groggily. "Just answer your phone."

I let out a sigh and rolled over to grab my phone. It was Kayla. It had been about two weeks since we had broken up and it would be another few days before she would go missing. Sarcastically, I answered the phone, "Ma'am, I believe you have the wrong number."

"*You're a fucking asshole, West,*" Kayla's voice cracked through the speaker.

"Well good morning to you, too," I replied sardonically.

"*It's four in the afternoon! You remember what you were supposed to do today?*" she asked. There was some kind of vitriolic righteousness in her voice. I scratched my head for a minute, trying to remember. Then it came to me.

"Oh, fuck, that was today, wasn't it?" I said.

"*Yeah, that was today.*"

"My bad. Had kind of a late night last night."

"*Let me guess – hungover?*"

"Try still drunk," I blurted out.

Kayla scoffed through the phone. "*I can't fucking believe you. I'm gonna go out on a limb and guess that you went home with some cheap bar whore last night and completely ignored the one thing I asked you to do today.*"

"Hey, I resent that," I rejoined, glancing at Izzy. "She isn't cheap." Izzy smacked me in the arm. "Besides," I went on, "did you really *need* me to drive you to the clinic? It's not like you can't get there yourself."

"*It's not about needing a ride,*" Kayla argued. "*It's about being supportive.*"

"Well fuck, I don't exactly need to be there when you fill the prescription. I can still be there for you when you take the pill."

"*You have absolutely no idea how stressful an abortion is, do you?*"

"That's not true. My mom tried to abort me when I was a baby. I mean, I was like six months old at the time but —"

Kayla cut me off. "*Is everything just a big fucking joke to you? I mean, what is this? You think this is funny?*"

"Everything is funny when you look at it the right way. Maybe in a couple of months we'll be able to sit down and laugh about all this." My attempt to justify my crass sense of humor did nothing to help me.

"*Fuck it, whatever. Don't come. I don't care anymore. You're the one who knocked me up in the first place, you shouldn't be able to shirk your responsibility. The only other person I've even been able to tell about this is Robin. Do you have any idea how this feels?*"

I sighed. "You're right, you're right, I'm sorry... I'd love to help you kill our child," I remarked sarcastically and grinned to myself.

"*Fuck you, West. That old woman was right. You're the devil.*"

"Hey," I said. "Happy Mother's day."

A guttural sound of anger came from the phone before Kayla hung up. I let my phone fall from my hand off the side of the bed where it hit the floor with a loud thud. I wasn't sure why I had to be so difficult – I think a part of me wanted Kayla to keep the baby, just so we'd always have a reason to be in each other's lives. Izzy rolled over and looked at me. "What?" I asked innocently. "Was I too harsh?"

"Maybe a little bit," Izzy replied.

The springy, worn out mattress provided little comfort as I sat up. My apartment was small and shitty, but it was mine. An air conditioner desperately struggled to produce cold air from the bedroom window, making a god awful creaking and whining sound as it battled to carry on. "All she wants me to do is drive her to the fucking clinic to get the pill," I argued. "Call me an asshole all you want but I don't really see the need for emotional support with that." Instinctively, I grabbed a bottle of warm spiced rum from my nightstand and took a swig, letting it run down my throat, searing it like battery acid.

Izzy took the bottle from me and passed me a joint. "I don't think it's really about that," she said. "I think she just wants to know that you'll be there for her."

"I think I'd rather be here," I replied, sliding my hand down Izzy's side. Izzy and I had been friends for years. We'd been hooking up off and on for a while – she was actually the third woman I had fucked that week, though I hoped Izzy didn't know about the other two. We weren't an item, it was just a shitty feeling sneaking around someone's back like that. Izzy was my tattoo artist, responsible for putting the devil on my shoulder – a silhouette image of a horned figure mid-flight like a bat out of hell. I told her my heart belonged to Kayla but my body belonged to her and she ran with it. She was a sweet girl, if not a little fucked in the head in her own way. Her body was covered in art; hell, her body *was* art. My face leaned toward hers to kiss her. She pushed me back.

"I think I'd rather you brush your teeth first," Izzy stated. "Your breath is *rank*."

"Really? I thought the rum would have helped," I joked and then got out of bed and sauntered to the bathroom, brushed my teeth and my reflection caught my eye. The guy looking back at me looked weary, worse for wear. He looked like shit. Blue eyes dimmed from exhaustion and a scruffy beard that desperately needed a trim. It didn't really matter, though. Nobody leaves behind a beautiful corpse.

I walked back into the room. Izzy was getting dressed. "Where you going?" I asked. "I don't have to be at work for another hour."

"Well you see, West, there are these things called *other people*, and other people actually, believe it or not, have their own schedules and their own shit to do," Izzy chided with a cute little grin. "I gotta get goin'." She had a unique charm to her as she looked at me with her hair draped over one eye.

As she went to pull up her jeans, I came up behind her and slid my hands around her waist. "Looks like you could use a little help with that." I squeezed my hands around her hips and she bit her lip.

"Maybe a little," she said softly. My hand explored her body and found she was already ready to go. In a moment, she was bent over the bed and her body rocked in rhythm with mine until we both hit our climax. She pulled my hand up to her face and bit the tip of my thumb as we breathed heavily.

"Okay," I said, pulling myself out of her. "You're good to go."

Izzy laughed and pulled up her pants. "Just like that and you're kicking me out, huh? Tsk tsk," she clicked her tongue. "A tale as old as time."

Her words made me grin as I leaned in to kiss her. "Coming to the Hole in the Ground tonight?"

She batted her eyelashes at me and coyly replied, "We'll see."

After a minute she was gone. I stood in the shower, letting the hot water burn my skin and cleanse me of the night's debauchery. My thoughts drifted back to Kayla, to what I had said to her over the phone. Maybe it was cruel. Maybe it was called for. Who the fuck knew. All that mattered at that moment was how god damn angry I was about all of it. As my mind replayed my own failures, my fist shot out and struck the wall of the shower, cracking the tile as little pieces fell into the bathtub.

They swam in the hot water boiling at my feet and circled the drain. I didn't really know why I did it. All I knew was that girl fueled a fucking rage in me that could make the devil cry.

***

I walked to work. It was a short walk, less than ten minutes unless I took a detour to go blaze in the woods down the trail. Other than fucking, the walk to and back from work was about the only exercise that I got. As I stepped out of my apartment, I saw my neighbor struggling to carry her trash can. She was a woman probably about my age, had lived there since before I moved next door, and whom I had almost never spoken to.

"Hey," I said unenthusiastically with a wave. She waved back to me. I thought about helping her move the heavy trashcan to the curb, but I was already kind of buzzed and on track to be late for work, so I left her to her own devices.

The walk itself was usually pleasant. Unfortunately, though, being out in the open left you vulnerable to passersby. This time it was a very familiar police cruiser. I kept walking as the cruiser slowed down beside me.

"Fine afternoon, isn't it West?" the cop said to me. He was a man in his fifties with a gray buzzcut and a clean shave. He was the first cop to ever give me charges – disorderly conduct for fighting in school, then some driving related charges years later – and he hated my fucking guts.

"Sure is, Officer Sparks," I replied without turning my head. "You gonna arrest me for enjoying my walk?" Officer Bill Sparks was Kayla's father and the reason she stayed away from the Hole in the Ground for as many years as she did.

"That depends," Bill said. "Drunk in public is a misdemeanor, and going by that staggering walk I'd say you've already had a couple."

"It's pronounced 'swagger' and no, I haven't been drinking. I'm incredibly high right now, but I haven't been drinking," I lied.

"The devil's lettuce, huh?" Bill replied coyly. I knew he was just fucking with me but that didn't make it any less irritating.

"More like the angel's snow," I shot back.

"Oh yeah? Who's your supplier? Maybe I know him."

"I don't know, isn't sniffing out drugs more of a job for a pig?"

Bill's face twitched with anger. Bill said, "You know, for someone who's been beat up as much as you have, you sure speak like someone who's never been smacked in the fucking mouth."

"Are you threatening me, Sparky?" He hated that nickname.

"No, no, just a friendly observation."

"Well, if that'll be it for you, I'd very much like to not be having this conversation anymore, so fuck off. Sorry, fuck off *officer*."

"I'll leave you be, just consider this your daily reminder to stay away from my daughter."

"Just because you said that, I'm gonna fuck her even harder next time."

The look of wild fury in Bill's eyes was unbelievable. He even began to stop the car, but the radio went off before he could throw it in park. *"We've got a ninety-one at the gas station on Main and Second."*

A ninety-one was loitering, pretty standard fare for the small town of Matchstick. Bill grabbed the radio and said, "Dispatch, this is Unit seven-twenty-one, en route." He shot me a look and said, "I'll be seeing you, West," then drove off.

As per usual I got to work ten minutes late. Nothing out of the ordinary – one of the perks of being the boss' son is you can get away with some shit you might not be able to elsewhere.

"Hey, dad," I said flatly as I strolled into the bar ten after four.

"Hey, West," my father replied. "What time is it?"

I checked my phone. "'Bout a quarter past four, why?"

"Huh," he said with feigned surprise. "So you *do* know how to read a fuckin' clock? That's so weird, because I thought I told you to be here at four, so when four o'clock rolled around, I just assumed you missed that day at school where they taught you how to tell time."

"Yeah yeah," I waved him off. "Sorry, long morning."

My father was a large man – bigger than me, that's for damn sure. He wore a similar outfit – black shirt, blue jeans – and sported short, gray hair, a thick and equally gray beard, and tattoos all over his arms. He'd had an angel tattooed on his shoulder since I was a baby. I got the devil tattooed on mine just to fuck with him at first, but it was really more of an homage to the man who raised me. Below the angel were the numbers "1970 - 1998," an *in memoriam* to my late mother.

"Long morning?" he scoffed playfully as he wiped down the bar. "Since when do you get up in the morning?"

"Long afternoon," I grinned. The interior of the Hole in the Ground was just as much of a shitty eyesore as the outside was: old, hard wooden floors; outdated designs and color choices for the walls and trimmings; dim lights that barely cast a glow; a few tables lined along the walls; couple of broken windows that would never be fixed; and a long wooden bar snaking across the back wall with a mirror behind the liquor shelf, situated just behind the beer taps – a barrier between the customer and the endless supply of liquor on the other side. It was a divey shithole, but it was ours.

"Hey," my father said, "did you get the wire on the fryer fixed yet? I keep telling you that shit is an electrical fire waiting to happen."

"No, not yet," I replied carelessly.

My dad shook his head and rolled his eyes. "God damn it, Weston. I asked you to do *one* thing. Just slap some fucking electrical tape on it."

"If that's all that needs to be done then why don't you do it?"

"Because it's my fucking bar and I told *you* to do it. Now do you want me to knock the shit out of you or are you gonna go back there and do that now?"

"Fine, fine, chill," I said defensively.

"And keep your eye on the bar for a minute," my dad told me. "I've got to call up the distributor real quick."

"I think I can handle that."

He pushed through the back door to the patio with a cigarette in one hand and his phone in the other. "Hey, it's Jim...." his voice trailed off as the door shut behind him.

I stood there at the bar twiddling my thumbs and double checking stock just to kill time. A couple of the daytime crowd still straggled behind, mostly older, sadder fuckers who hit retirement and never picked up a hobby. After a few minutes, I decided to go ahead and perform the one task my father asked of me.

The kitchen was small, only containing a fryer, a small grill, and a sink. Painstakingly, I pulled the fryer out a few feet until I could see the exposed wire in the back. Electric tape in hand, I cautiously wrapped it around the wire, careful not to touch the exposed wire because I was too lazy to unplug the fucking thing beforehand. The wire was surrounded by what I presumed was highly flammable insulation material sticking out from the walls, exposed from years of neglect and disrepair around the base of the kitchen walls. Just as I was about to finish, the sound of a voice hollering, "Hey bartender!" loudly from the other room startled me. My finger brushed against the wire and gave me a good shock. "Fuck!" I shouted as I waved my hand in pain. "Fuck it, good enough," I huffed as I pushed the fryer back into place. "Now who the fuck – oh, god damn it, of course it was you."

Clyde stood there grinning with Izzy beside him.

"Congrats," I began, "you managed to be even later than I was."

"Yeah," Clyde began. "My fucking car broke down again. God damn head gasket." He shook his head and clicked his tongue in irritation. "I'd have better luck getting a fucking bike."

"Good luck getting women to go home with you on a bicycle," I laughed. "'Hey girl,'" I mimicked, "'wanna hop on the big wheel? Baby's a ten-speed.'"

Clyde let out a laugh and said, "Bet I could pull it off."

Izzy sat down at the bar. "Hey man, chicks dig big wheels. I'd go home with a guy on a bike."

"You'd go home with anybody," I teased. We shot each other knowing glances.

"You wish," she grinned. "Lemme get a shot of Crown before I dip."

"Smart girl," I joked. "Just like that song, 'have a drink, have a drive.'"

Izzy laughed. "Don't worry, it's a short drive."

"Yeah," Clyde agreed, "telephone pole's right up the street. You'll hit it in no time."

"Don't jinx me, asshole!" she exclaimed as I set the shot down in front of her.

"Isabella," Clyde replied, "you *are* the jinx."

She downed the shot and said, "Damn right, momma didn't raise no bitch. Well, she did, but his name is Clyde."

I laughed out loud and Clyde looked at her with challenge in his eyes and a bit of a smirk and said, "I'll remember you said that."

"On that note," Izzy stated, "I'm outta here. Text me if you need a ride home."

"Oh, I will. Just so you can have the satisfaction of telling me no," Clyde jested.

"Good," Izzy grinned. She looked at me then said, "See ya, Superman." That had been her nickname for me for a while.

"See ya, Tinker Bell," I replied with a small grin. She blew me a kiss in a deliberately exaggerated fashion then turned to walk out the door. I watched her as she went, my eyes fixated on her swaying hips and the yoga pants tightly hugging her ass. Clyde took notice.

"Stop eye-fucking my sister, god dammit," he said, only half kidding.

"My bad," I chuckled.

"Look man," he held his hand out, still kind of grinning but there was a serious undertone behind it, "you can fuck any stray piece of ass in the god forsaken town of Matchstick all you want, but if you touch my sister, I'll knock your fucking teeth down your throat."

My feet shifted uncomfortably in place and I said to Clyde, "Nah, man. I wouldn't do that to you."

Chapter 3

The night went about as expected. Crowd shuffled in until 9:30 then stabilized. Music was loud, lights were low, people were laughing and making noise. I knew damn near everybody in there. You hang around a small town like Matchstick long enough and you start to know people. Not just names and faces, but secrets. You know who did what, who has which illegal substance on them, who's supplying and who's buying. You know who fucked who the night before and you know when their significant others find out about it. In some ways, you know more about these people than you even know about yourself, and that's a scary fucking reality to be in.

Jane, the other bartender who worked the Hole, sat on the client side of the bar enjoying her night off. "Can I get another beer, West?" she asked me over the noise.

As I walked by, I pretended like I didn't see her and asked the patrons sitting next to her, "Did you guys need another drink? You need another round?"

Jane laughed and said, "Fuck off." I grinned at her and poured her a fresh drink. Jane was a sweetheart but she could throw down with the best of them. She had a lot of patience but when someone pushed her to her limit and the gloves came off, someone was walking out of there with a black eye.

It was around 11:30 when I got off work, after the crowd began to thin out a little, finally able to have myself a fucking drink. Dad stayed behind the bar, never getting weeded, never getting overwhelmed, never showing a single sign of stress.

"Can you pour me a Captain and coke? I gotta take a piss." I asked him as I rounded over to the client side of the bar. A few girls sat there coyly flirting with him. My father had aged gracefully, apparently, because he seemed to attract the attention of many of the younger women who came through.

"Sure," he replied as he turned his attention back to the girls.

I pushed through the wooden door of the men's room – just as shitty as the rest of the building, with two barely functioning urinals and a toilet that's seen the worst of humanity – and went to open the stall door, badly vandalized with inane graffiti and barely legible carvings into the wood. It was unlocked, but someone was in there.

"Shit, my bad," I said.

"You're good, bud." It was a regular named Johnny, a young local kid who was barely twenty-one, but had been going to the Hole for a few months. He came out of the stall without flushing the toilet and I went in after him, expecting to see a bowl full of pisswater. Instead, there was a little plastic baggy in the water and a short straw on top of the toilet. "Mother fucker…." I muttered. Thoughts ran through my head as I decided what I would do next for a second, then grabbed the straw and followed Johnny out of the bathroom.

"Hey," I grabbed him by the shoulder. "You forgot something."

Johnny turned around and his eyes lit up as I held the coke straw in front of him. He shrugged and said, "That's not mine, bro."

"Bullshit," I replied, tossing the straw into a trashcan near us. "I don't care what you do in your free time, but don't be bringing that shit into my bar, okay?"

"Bro, it's not mine," he argued again.

"Don't bullshit me, Johnny. I'm not kicking you out, I'm just giving you a warning, alright? I got you. Just don't do it again."

"Alright, alright, word," he finally said. Johnny was known for his white powder habit, same as a few other regulars. Johnny did blow with Trent and Cal, got it from Bailey who got his from Fletch. Fletch was a man in his mid-thirties with a vacant stare and permanently slurred speech, sitting at the bar with a girl who couldn't have been a day over twenty-one. My father was carding her as I walked over. I didn't like Fletch, but I had my eyes on him. We all knew he was a worm, but we couldn't do anything until we proved what we already knew. Clyde sat at the bar, taking a well deserved night off and passively keeping his eye on the crowd. My father could handle most any trouble, but Clyde and I would be more than willing to step in if it were called for. I stood next to him in front of the taps, catching my reflection in the mirror behind the liquor shelves. Clyde sat on a barstool with a small pile of cash in front of him.

"Careful," he said, holding his hand over the money. "That's my ex-girlfriend's money." He grinned a little. Clyde was even more well known for his debauchery than I was. If you were at the Hole, chances were that at least a couple of the women there on any given night had fucked him at some point.

"Wait, really?" I asked, looking at the money on the bar. At that moment, I felt the strange sensation of long acrylic nails poking my side.

"Excuuuuuuse me," a woman's voice said.

I looked over my shoulder and saw a girl I knew in passing named Tanya – the aforementioned ex-girlfriend of Clyde's from a brief fling a few months back. She pushed her way between me and him then looked at me with a drunken stare, somewhere between recognition and recollection and held her hand out. "Hi," she said. "I'm Tanya."

As I shook her hand, I said, "Yeah, I know. We've met. A couple of times."

She laughed then turned back to Clyde, slowly pushing herself more and more onto him until she sat in his lap. Every time she moved her ass bumped into my leg and I would move a little further away. I couldn't hear what they were saying, but I got the impression they weren't saying much as she put her mouth over his and they started to make out at the bar. I stared up at the ceiling for a minute until they finally relented, she said something to him, then walked off.

There was a brief moment of silence, then Clyde and I both broke into laughter. "She seems like a charming girl," I said.

"Yeah, and her boyfriend is somewhere around here," Clyde said humorously as he looked around.

I laughed again and Clyde gave me a look to say he was being serious. "Wait, that's a joke, right?"

"Nah man, her boyfriend is *actually* here." He laughed again. "I think he wants me to fuck her."

"Welcome to the fucking future," I replied with an eyeroll. "Every man is either a cuck or in therapy. We might just be the last of the old world."

"Yeah, I'm not doing that," Clyde laughed again. "Fucking unbelievable."

A man I didn't recognize came up to us and said brightly to Clyde, "Hey, man! Long time no see!"

Clyde shook his hand and cheerfully said, "Hey, bro, how are you? It's been a minute. You good?"

"Yeah man, life is alright."

"Hey man, keep it up," Clyde replied.

The man raised his glass and said, "Will do!" and then walked off.

Clyde watched him walk away and then said to me, "I have *no* fucking idea who that is."

I howled with laughter. "Are you serious?"

"Yeah," Clyde cackled. "Never met him before in my life."

"Just roll with the punches, right?"

My father came over and said, "Hey Clyde, where'd your girlfriend go? She owes me money for her tab."

"She's not my girlfriend, Jim," Clyde protested. "But I'm pretty sure this cash is for you." He slid the money over to Jim.

My father looked at it and said, "That's great, she's only about ninety fucking dollars short."

"That sounds more like her problem than mine," Clyde shrugged as Jim walked over to another group of drinkers.

"Holy hell, man, you sure know how to pick them."

"I swear to god, I can't leave my house without something weird happening. You know why I put a slot machine sticker on my door?"

"Why?"

"Because every time I go through that door I'm taking a fucking gamble. No matter what, even if I'm just sitting here minding my own business, *something* is gonna happen. Some drunk chick that I used to bang will come up and start trying to sleep with me again, some dude I've never met is gonna try and start a fight, something's gonna catch on fire. It's always *something*."

I shrugged and said, "Hey man, at least we're living lives worth living, right? Most people can't honestly say that."

"You know what it is? It's the universe. If you ask the universe to start giving you experiences, it will. You've just got to ask."

"Huh," I hummed. I thought about all of the circumstances that led me to Kayla. "Is there any way to ask it to stop?"

Clyde rose from his seat and said, "That's the thing, though – do we really want it to stop?" then grabbed his drink and wandered outside.

Those words went around in my head for a while. Do we really want it to stop? Kayla and I had failed and tried again at a relationship half a dozen times and yet we still kept coming back. It was a nightmarish ride that never seemed to end, but maybe that was because neither of us were ever quite ready for it to end.

After a few minutes, I grabbed my own drink from the bar and made my way out back to chain smoke and drink myself into a stupor. The acrid smell of burning plastic hit my nose as soon as I was out the door.

"What the fuck is that?" I asked.

Clyde, whose face was also one of disgust, nodded over to one of the picnic tables where a few people I knew were burning plastic and trash in an ashtray. "I believe that's the problem," he said with a morbid chuckle.

"Jesus fucking christ," I rolled my eyes.

"That smells like absolute shit," a girl standing nearby said, pinching her nose.

There was a mostly empty cup of ice and water sitting on the table closest to me, so I picked it up and walked over to the group with the fire. "Oh cool, you guys having a little fire pit?" I asked.

"Why yes we are," one of them replied.

"Cool, cool," I said, then immediately turned the cup of water upside down over the fire and put it over the ashtray. "Aw, what happened? Your fire pit went out."

"Dammit, West!" one of them yelled. I laughed to myself and sauntered away.

A few of my friends stood around another one of the picnic tables outside. "Seriously," one named Zach was saying, "where the hell are all the fine ass bitches tonight? It's a fucking sausage fest out here, bro."

"They saw you comin' and they ran," another friend named Greg replied.

"He's got a point," I added as I joined the conversation. "I don't think I've ever actually *seen* you with a woman," I laughed.

"Shit, man, I do alright," Zach defended. "Besides, Kayla was about the finest piece of ass I've ever seen you with and you done scared her off, so…"

"A fine piece of ass *you'll* never get," I retorted. I could feel my temperature rising as that little voice of anger in the back of my head got a bit louder.

"Well shit, if you're done with her then feel free to send her my way," Zach laughed. "I'll happily make her squirt a couple times then kick her ass to the curb."

The faces of the people around us all wore expressions like they knew someone had just fucked up. Carefully, I set my drink down on the table, took a drag from my cigarette, and said with a wicked grin: "That right?"

Zach also grinned nervously, unsure how to take me. "Shit, I mean –"

I didn't let him finish his sentence. Before the next syllable was out my fist had already shot out and slammed into the center of his torso. He stumbled back into the picnic table and caught himself as he fell, then launched toward me from the table and swung his fist, striking me in the jaw.

"Knock it the fuck off!" Clyde yelled as he jumped in between me and Zach. "West, go sit somewhere else," he commanded. "Zach, you're done for the night. Go pay your tab and get the fuck out."

"I didn't even fucking do anything!" Zach argued back.

"I don't give a shit," Clyde argued back, not receding by an inch. He pointed toward the door. "Go pay your tab and get the fuck out." Clyde was a fighter, but didn't matter if he was working or not; he made it his mission to quell violence more than to cause it.

"Fuck this place," Zach muttered. "And fuck your girlfriend," he said as he pointed at me.

Quickly, I moved toward him to throw another fist but Clyde put his hand on my chest to stop me. "I swear to god, West, I will knock you the fuck out." With the situation defused, I sat there and drank my drinks trying to shake off the rage. By the time the bar had closed and cleared out, I was still thinking about it. It was just me and my father in the bar by then as he counted the register and I flipped the stools.

"Need me for anything else?" I asked, eager to get home and keep drinking.

"No, you're good. Why don't you sit down for a minute, though?" Jim said in his gravelly voice, cracked from years of shouting and drinking and smoking.

"What for?" I asked.

"I want to talk to you."

"About?"

"Sit the fuck down and you'll find out."

Begrudgingly, I listened. I pulled down one of the barstools and sat across from my father as he stood on the other side of the bar. He pulled out a couple of rocks glasses, put a few ice cubes in them, then withdrew a bottle of scotch from beneath the bar. "Macallan?" I asked. "Isn't that shit expensive?"

"Unbelievably expensive."

"Since when the fuck do we serve that?"

"We don't," he answered as he poured a shot into each of the glasses.. "It's my personal supply." He slid one of the glasses toward me. I took it and sipped the decade-plus old scotch. It was a smooth burn. "Do you remember my grandma – your great grandma Libby?" he asked me out of nowhere.

My finger scratched my head for a minute. "Yeah, I think so. Didn't she die years ago?"

"She did, God rest her soul," he responded. "She told me a story one time, I don't know if it was true or not but the way she told it was. We had an ancestor, years and years back, probably around the turn of the century. He was a gambler. Got in with all sorts of the wrong people. You know the type. Well, the story goes that he was pretty bad down on his luck one time, asked God for some help and God didn't answer, so he asked the Devil instead. Told the Devil he just needed one big win then he was done, he was set, and his soul would belong to the Devil. Well, I guess someone must have heard his prayers 'cause he won big that night. Won more money than he'd ever seen in his life before. Then he kept going. Kept playing. Eventually, he lost all that money. Lost it to a better gambler in a game of cards, and he wanted it back. He left the casino or the bar or wherever the hell he was, got back up on his horse, drunker than piss, and followed the man who beat him when he left. He was ready to kill him."

I clung onto my father's every word, partly out of interest and partly out of confusion. He kept going.

"Couple minutes into the ride, his horse starts acting funny. Throwing its head. Kicking its hooves. Acting like it was scared of something. He can't figure out what it is. Then all of a sudden he feels a weight behind him like someone else is on the fuckin' horse. He feels heat – not like a warm body, like a fuckin' furnace – all down his back. Horse takes off running, shoots right past the man he's following. He's scared out of his mind, turns around to look what's behind him and he sees this big, black, looming apparition of a figure with what he swore were horns. His back starts burning. Horse ran so fast he got back home before he knew it. Got home and passed out. Story goes when he woke up, his wife said he had a burn on his back in the shape of the devil."

I let his words hang in the air as I sipped my scotch, then finally said: "So you're telling me your grandma was crazy."

"That's the point, West. Our family is fucking crazy and has been for generations. Your grandma's maiden name is *Moody* for Christ's sake. You've gotta be careful. You're twenty-six years old now, you can't be throwing punches every time someone says some shit that you don't like. That's how you end up in prison or end up dead."

"Well," I said flatly, finishing my drink and jumping to my feet, "great story. But I'm not gonna end up in prison. You don't have to worry. I don't think I've done anything too crazy…yet."

My father shook his head and sighed as I walked away. "You know how that story ended?" he asked as I reached the door. I turned back to look at him. "The next day he found the man and killed him. Never got his money back and he killed himself in prison." My father gave me a long stare. "Your great grandma said we've still got the devil on our backs. And you've gotta be careful what you ask him for."

Chapter 4

My thoughts wandered all around me as I laid in my bed at night. Kayla and I had gone through falling outs a few times, but this last one seemed permanent. My mind drifted back to how it happened.

We were at a bar called Julia's Tavern one night a few weeks ago. Clyde was with us, and so was Kayla's best friend, Robin. We all stood outside smoking and carrying on as we imbibed our drinks.

"It would be interesting to see you two fight," Kayla said to me and Clyde.

We both kind of chuckled and I asked, "Why's that?"

Kayla shrugged. "You guys are about the same size, you're always out drinking, Idunno. It would just be interesting to see."

Clyde shot me a mischievous grin. "Wanna find out?" he asked.

I laughed and said, "I'm pretty sure I wouldn't win that one, babe. Clyde practically fights for a living." Kayla laughed and then turned her attention back to Robin. I said to Clyde, "For real, though, let's hope it never comes to that."

"Hey, man, I've never had a friend whose ass I didn't kick at *some* point," he chortled.

"Well I certainly hope that isn't true 'cause then there's a lot of people you're gonna have to fight," I laughed as I heard the voice of a man talking to Kayla and her friends.

"Can I buy you another orange crush?" he asked, noticing Kayla's half empty orange drink.

"Thanks but I'm good," Kayla replied politely as I listened from a few yards away.

"I buy all the pretty girls drinks," he pressed. "Don't worry about it."

Robin said, "I'll take one or two," and laughed.

"It's okay, I'm here with my boyfriend." As if on cue, I sauntered over.

"What's up?" I asked Kayla.

The man answered for her. "Just seeing if any of these pretty ladies wanted a drink."

"Sure," I said. "She'll take one. So will I."

The man laughed uncomfortably and said, "I really just buy drinks for the ladies. You get it, right man?"

As he laughed, I did too, and said, "Nah, I get it." Then I held my hand out to shake his. "I'm West. What's your name, man?"

Amicably, he took my hand and shook it. "I'm Dan, nice to meet you."

"Likewise." My head turned and looked at Kayla. "Hey, I'm gonna go in and get another drink, I'll be right back." Gave her a little peck on the lips then went inside and stood at the bar waiting for Paul the bartender to serve me.

"Another round?" he asked.

"Actually," I began, "Dan said he wanted to buy me and my girlfriend a round. Two orange crushes on his tab."

Paul looked past me out the door at Dan standing over by Kayla and her friends. "Really? You wanna go grab him real quick?"

I looked back through the door then turned my head back to Paul and said, "He said he likes to buy girls' drinks," with a shrug. "Said he does it all the time."

"Well, yeah, that's true," Paul said. "Two orange crushes you said?"

"Please."

After a minute, she handed me the drinks and I stepped back outside, held them in the air, and said, "Hey, Dan, thanks for the drinks!" Kayla took one and I kept the other for myself as he watched me with an irritated expression. But I knew he wouldn't do anything about it so he didn't look like a cheap fuck to all the other girls.

As the night began to draw to a close, I asked Kayla: "Coming back to my place tonight?"

"That's the plan," she said. "I have to stop at the Hole first, though. I left my phone charger there last night."

I checked the time and said, "They're gonna be closed by now. My dad never stays open past twelve-thirty on weekdays."

"Can I borrow your key, then?" she said. "I'll just be in and out."

"Alright," I replied, handing her the key to the bar, "just let me know when you're on your way over. I'm getting out of here." Then I leaned in and kissed her. "I love you."

Slowly, I got drunker and drunker as I sat in my living room with a bottle of jack and a coke to chase it, just waiting for Kayla to get there. After an hour had passed, I tried calling her. Straight to voicemail – guess she hadn't charged her phone yet. Then I started getting mad, getting angry, growing concerned, wondering where she was. My thoughts turned to the possibility that she had gone home with someone at Julia's Tavern, maybe that orange crush guy. Or that she was meeting someone and was hiding it from me. The thought of her cheating drove me to fury; she had fucked around on me once before almost a year ago and I took her back like a fool. She got hers, so I would get mine. I texted Izzy: "You wanna come over?"

With my phone in my hand, I passed out waiting for a response.

The next morning I woke up with a text from Kayla. It just said, "Babe," with a frowny face after it.

"How come you didn't come over last night?" I asked. I was just waiting for the admission of guilt. There was no doubt in my mind that she had gotten drunk and fucked some guy last night and now she going to play the apology card.

"Something bad happened last night," she texted back.

My heart sank. "What happened?"

"I think I have a concussion."

"A concussion? How did you get a concussion?"

"I fell," she texted.

"What? How? When?" Despite my efforts, I couldn't hide my skepticism.

The three dots that indicate someone is typing appeared, then disappeared, then reappeared again for several minutes. The anxiety was killing me. So I took a shot while waiting for her explanation.

Finally, it came. "I got mugged leaving the Hole last night," she said.

The blood in my body froze so fast that the shards of ice could have cut me from inside my veins. "Are you okay?" I asked, quickly followed by, "Call me." After fifteen seconds I called her. She didn't answer. Called her again. Still, no answer. "Please call me."

She texted me back. "I was leaving the Hole and someone came up to me at my car, knocked me out and took all the money from my purse."

As I read her words, I didn't know what to do. A part of me was still skeptical, but another part of me was *hoping* it was a lie just so that I wouldn't have to live with the knowledge that someone attacked her and I wasn't there to defend her. "Are you home?" I asked.
"Yeah."

"I'm coming over." I didn't wait for a response. Quickly, I threw on my clothes, brushed my teeth, then hurried outside into my car and drove over there, seething for the entire fifteen minute drive because I didn't believe her for a second. Muggings didn't happen like that in Matchstick. She was fucking around on me and I knew it.

My car came to a stop in front of her apartment and she was already sitting outside ready to greet me with a forlorn look on her face. I was ready to grill her, to interrogate her about what happened until she let the truth slip.

And then I saw her face.

She had a burst blood vessel in her eye right by the bridge of her nose. If you've ever spent time watching fights or getting into them, then you know what that burst blood vessel is from. It's caused by being hit really fucking hard around the orbital of the skull.

She was telling the truth.

Without a word, I put my arms around her and held her there in the spring breeze. She said nothing. She didn't cry. She didn't break. She held it together. "I'm sorry," I whispered.

The next few nights would be spent at Kayla's place. I wasn't sure if it was her who didn't want to be alone or if it was me. Either way, we spent more time together those couple of days than we ever had before. I sat on my computer right next to her bed as she lay there ready to go to sleep. She put her hand on my arm and looked at me with a smile.

"What?" I asked with a grin.

"Nothing," she said smiling. "I just like having you here. I wish you could just move in."

"I'll do it," I said immediately. "My lease is up in a couple months. I can come live here with you."

"You would actually do that?" she asked.

"I would do anything for you." I stared deeply into her chocolate brown eyes and felt the love that was still there between us. "Besides," I shrugged, "you're pretty decent company. I dare say I think I kinda like you," I teased.

Kayla laughed and said softly, "I think I kinda like you, too."

I wished I could have stayed in that moment; wished we could have stayed like that forever. Not at each other's throats. Not fighting. Not distrusting. All we did was laugh, hold each other, and fuck like a pair of rabbits trying to save their species. Just love, through and through. It was the saddest dream that I ever had – the dream that we could hold onto that feeling. But reality catches up to everyone soon enough.

After a few days, it was finally time to leave. "I like having you here," Kayla said, "but I do need my own space. You know? I haven't really processed what happened, I think I've been using you as sort of an emotional buffer."

"You're okay," I told her. "I understand. Take all the time that you need. I'll be around. I'm always here for you – forever."

I didn't hear from her for an entire day and a half after that. Then, she texted me and asked, "Hey, can we talk?"

"Sure. Meet me at Julia's?" Kayla understandably avoided the Hole after the assault and battery. I wasn't sure what she wanted to talk about, but after the last few days all of my anxieties about losing her had been washed away. So I met her at Julia's and sat down beside her.

"What's up?" I asked my girlfriend as Paul made me a drink. Kayla had only a water.

"First off, I just wanted to thank you for being there for me the last few days. You really made it easier to handle what happened."

"Of course. I'm here for you, and I always will be."

Kayla recoiled slightly. "That's kind of what I wanted to talk about."

"Oh?" My heart sank but I tried to keep it off my face.

Kayla brushed her hand through her long, dark hair. "I don't know how I feel about *forever*," she began. "I mean, I'm only twenty-five years old. I have a lot of life left to live. I don't want to be in Matchstick forever, and I know you don't have any plans of leaving here any time soon."

"I mean, all of my friends are here," I replied, sort of confused and highly anxious. My drink couldn't kick in fast enough.

"I know, and that's fine, you know? I don't want to pressure you into doing something you don't want to. I just know that this isn't the right place for me. I'm not ready to settle down yet."

"Settle down?" I asked, my voice rising. "Nobody's asking you to settle down. I mean, I'm not exactly over here popping the question or trying to put a baby in you."

"I know, I know, but still," she went on to my chagrin, "I don't think I'm ready for something long term. I'm not ready for that kind of commitment. I want to be fair to you, you know?"

My blood went from frozen to boiling over in an instant. "Are you fucking serious?" I asked.

"West, I'm sorry but – "

"Oh, yeah, fucking sorry, sure," I shouted. People began to look at us. "This must be so goddamn difficult for you. I would fucking do anything for you, Kayla. You really want to throw that away?"

"Anything?" she asked, her own voice rising. "Would you stop drinking?"

Mother fucker. She already knew the answer. "That depends," I shirked the question. "Are you asking me to?"

"No," she replied, "but I don't think that you would."

"I work at a *bar*, of course I fucking drink."

"See, this is my point, West. You always have some kind of excuse. You're somehow blameless in your own problems. I can't be with someone like that."

"Really? Because it was working out pretty fucking fine two days ago!" I yelled. "Nah, nah, I should have seen this coming. It's only the fifth fucking time it's happened. I'm sick of this shit. You are so *unbelievably* full of shit, Kayla."

"You don't have to be a child about this, West. You could be civil and we can be adults."

"Fuck that and fuck you, too," I roared as I downed my drink and rose to my feet. I pulled a five out of my wallet and slapped it onto the bar. "You're a bad person, Kayla. You do shitty things to people. And you get what you fucking deserve."

Kayla just shook her head, unafraid of my tirade. "Focus on you, West. Take care of your health, okay? We shouldn't have gotten back together, I'm sorry that I had to put you through this."

"Fuck that. We should have never dated in the first place. I wish I had just turned right back around when I saw you at the bar that first time." I walked over to the door, opened it, then turned back around as Kayla called out my name.

"West, please don't make it like this," she pleaded with tears in her eyes. I didn't know what it was, but something was fucking eating her and I wasn't privy to it. Suddenly I wondered how much about the woman I didn't know. "This hurts me, too. I just... I just can't be with you." Tears streamed from her eyes down her cheeks.

I stared at her for a moment and contemplated going back and talking things through. Thought about asking what was wrong, what was going on in her life behind closed doors because I knew there was something. Instead, I said: "Just do me a favor. Don't fucking come back this time. I'm tired of living in the past."

One week later she would tell me she was pregnant.

A couple weeks after that she would be missing.

And the people would remember what I had said to her.

Chapter 5

It was a slow night as I stood at the bar serving drinks. I had only a handful of patrons by ten o'clock. Izzy sat at one end of the bar and Fletch sat at the other, beer dripping from his long tangled beard, with a dozen or so drinkers in between them.

"West, get me another one," he said with slightly slurred words. I wasn't sure if he was shit faced or had a speech impediment.

"I'm not your goddamn servant, Fletch. What's the magic word?"

Fletch rolled his eyes and said, "Please, may I have another fucking beer?"

A grin spread across my face and I said facetiously, "Sure thing, buddy," as I set the beer down in front of him then went over to talk with Izzy as she scrolled through her phone, sipping on her drink. "Need another round, beautiful?"

"Golly mister, you really think I'm beautiful?" she joked.

"Tinker Bell, you're as beautiful as a starry sky and as gay as the sunrise."

"I always knew the sunrise was a fag," she laughed. "How are things with Kayla? You guys patch things up yet?"

"Why? Afraid I'm gonna drop you?"

Izzy smirked and said, "You always do, eventually."

I put my hand over my heart and made a mocking expression of pain. "That hurts, Izzy. That hurts real deep." She laughed. I continued. "But no, I haven't talked to her since the other day on the phone. She stopped coming here after she got robbed. I haven't seen her in days."

"That's understandable," Izzy said empathetically. "Besides, if she came here she'd have to see *you*, and none of us ever want to do that," she teased.

"Damn, I really feel the love in the air tonight," I laughed. Sometimes I wondered if there could be something real with me and Izzy. She had been in abusive relationships before and I always felt like that was something that terrified her with forming new ones. Her last ex used to treat her like shit. He would berate her, insult her, lie and cheat. It all came to a head, though, when he pushed her down the stairs.

Izzy called me after midnight the night that it happened. *"Hey, are you home?"*

"I'm at the Hole, why?"

She sniffled through the phone. *"I need to get out of here but I'm too fucked up to drive."*

"What happened?"

There was silence for a moment, then she said, *"He pushed me down the stairs."*

"What?!" I exclaimed, then remembered I was on the phone with her and didn't want to blow out her eardrum. "Are you okay?" I wanted to kill him, and so would a lot of other people if they knew, but the most important thing was being there for her – not being her avenger.

"Yeah, I'm okay. Can you pick me up?"

"I'll be there in a few minutes."

As I sat in my car waiting for her, I could hear her abuser yelling at her to come back. But she didn't listen, and got in my car just like I hoped she would. I took her to go stay with her parents just outside of town.

"Everybody thinks I'm this great person but I'm not," she said through watery eyes. "I've done shitty things to a lot of people. I'm not perfect."

"No," I said, "you're not perfect. And believe me, I know all about doing shitty things to people and making bad decisions. But it's kinda part of your charm."

Izzy laughed warmly. "Thank you, West. Thank you for getting me out of there, for listening. Thank you for being a friend." She hugged me tightly for a long time. I was okay with it. Finally, she let me go and asked, "How do I look?"

"Like you've been crying," I teased.

She laughed softly again then opened the passenger door and said, "I'll call you tomorrow, okay?"

We met up for drinks the next night at a bar about twenty minutes outside of town, mostly to avoid having to see any people that we knew. I gave her twenty dollars to put in the jukebox and the songs she picked were so in sync with what I would have chosen that it was almost eerie. "*If I go crazy then will...*"

As the jukebox blared, I looked at Izzy with a grin and said, "Will you?"

"Will I what?"

"Still call me Superman. That's the question in the song. He's asking her if she'll still call him Superman if he goes crazy."

She smiled and replied, "I'm not worried about you going crazy, West."

"Maybe you should be."

Izzy's grin slowly faded as she looked at me. I think she realized there was a seriousness beneath the question. It wasn't just a cute romantic thing. I really wanted to know. I *needed* to know.

"Will you?"

Izzy's smile slowly returned as she looked me in the eyes and said, "Of course I will, Superman."

We had a great time that night, and after a few beers, I invited her back to my apartment, not sure what would happen and unconcerned with the consequences.

She followed me in her car and as we went down a long, straight road in the back country with only a few houses along it, something happened that would bond us in a way I couldn't have foreseen.

I watched her headlights in my rearview mirror as they swerved off the side of the road and went out. My heart stopped almost as fast as my car did. Within moments, I was outside and full on sprinting toward her, calling her name and fearing the worst. As I got closer, I could see what happened. She had veered just slightly off the road, but enough to collide head on with a telephone pole, snapping it in half at the base. Her car was mangled; smoke poured from beneath the hood. Terrified, I pulled open her door. Smoke flooded the inside of the car and Izzy sat there dazed, but unharmed.

"Shit," she said quietly. "I'm sorry."

"Fuck being sorry, are you *okay*?" I asked with relief.

"I think so, yeah." She unfastened her seatbelt and began picking up her things from the floor. I wasn't sure what to do next. Then, the resident of one of those houses came outside with a flashlight.

"Hey, are you guys okay?" he called out.

Fuck. Had to think quickly. "Yeah," I replied. "Deer ran across the road."

"Want me to call an ambulance?" the man shouted.

"No, no, nobody's hurt, but thank you." Shit, shit, shit.

"You sure?" he asked suspiciously.

"Yes, thank you."

"We really should call somebody…." he said more to himself than me.

I glanced around really quick and said to Izzy, "Look, we need to get out of here *now*. If this asshole calls someone, they'll bring the police, you'll get a DUI and so will I. We can *not* let that happen. I don't care if I get another one but I'll be damned if I let it happen to you. So we're going to leave your car here and go back to my place. The police will almost definitely tow your car, and you might get charged with leaving the scene of an accident, but trust me – I've been arrested for both of those things and a DUI is *far* more severe."

"Okay," Izzy replied, still in a daze. I took her hand and pulled her out of her car, then we both walked as quickly as possible back to my car and took off like a bat out of hell. When we got back to my apartment, we just sat in the back seat of my car for a while.

Izzy cried softly and wrapped her arms around me. "I'm so sorry. I wanted to have a good time with you tonight."

"It's okay. You have nothing to be sorry for. I'm just glad that you're okay."

"You really make me feel safe..." she said. "I appreciate it so much. You probably saved me from a fucking DUI back there." She paused for a moment, then said, "I'll definitely try to make it up to you. You really are my Superman."

I smiled at her and said, "Always will be. And if I needed you to make it up to me, then I wouldn't be your Superman, now would I?" We smiled at each other deeply and affectionately. After a few seconds, Izzy put her lips against mine and we made love for the first time – a euphemism that I do not use lightly.

When I looked at Izzy sitting in the bar, I remembered that night. As my thoughts drifted through memories, a guy I knew in passing walked in named Vince, pulling me back to reality. He was short and stocky, built like a brawler with short hair and a chinstrap beard. He walked up to me by the beer taps. "What're you drinking, Vince?"

"I'm good, actually. Is Fletch here?" he asked distantly.

"Yeah," I replied, pointing my thumb down to the other end of the bar. "He's in his usual spot."

Vince turned his head and saw Fletch, then immediately walked over to him. Sensing trouble brewing, I followed from behind the bar.

"Hey, bitch," Vince said angrily. Fletch looked up from his phone with an expression of surprise. "The fuck you think you're doing?" Vince asked. He got in Fletch's face. "That girl you had here the other night? Maisy? Ring any fuckin' bells?"

Fletch feigned trying to remember, then nodded his head. "Yeah, I know her. What about it?"

"Bro, that's my *sister*. She's only fucking seventeen, bro. You're like thirty-five, what the fuck do you think you're doing with my seventeen year old sister?"

I chimed in at the revelation. "What the fuck, Fletch? You brought an underager into the fucking bar?"

Fletch recoiled defensively. "I didn't know she wasn't twenty-one. She had a fake ID."

"Bro, you *gave* her the fake ID! You've been having her fuck you for fucking coke, bro. She's been fucking fiending for days."

Fletch just kinda shook his head and threw his hand up. "I don't know what to tell you, man. I didn't give her *any* of that shit."

Vince leaned in real close and began shouting. "You stay away from my fucking sister, got me? Don't be sniffing around her anymore, don't be giving her drugs and getting her fucked up, and don't you *ever* fucking touch her again or I swear to god I'll put your dick in the dirt." Vince was ready to go to blows. A man that angry was a dangerous thing. I didn't know if he was going to beat

Fletch half to death or get him all the way there, but I was damn sure it wasn't going to happen on my watch. My father kept a handgun tucked away under the bar; I didn't think I would need it, but it was there if I did.

"Fuck off, man," Fletch said. Then the levee broke. Vince fist swung out and rocked Fletch in the jaw. He fell from his stool and Vince descended onto him. Immediately, I jumped over the bar and pulled Vince off the man.

"That's enough!" I shouted as I finally wrestled Vince away from him. "Vince, let him up."

Panting, Vince stood back. He pointed a finger at Fletch and said, "If I see you around her again, I'll fucking kill you."

Vince looked at me and I asked, "You good, man?"

"Yeah, I'm good."

"Why don't you go on home," I stated, putting my hand on his shoulder. "I've got my eye on Fletch. He brings your sister here again, he'll never set foot in the Hole ever again. Okay?"

Vince breathed deeply and said, "Okay, man. I gotchu." Then he turned and walked out the door.

I went over and helped pull Fletch to his feet. "You alright?" I asked. "Looks like he got you pretty fuckin' good."

"Yeah, I'm fine," Fletch replied. "Thanks."

"Don't be doing that shit again, got me? I'm not gonna bar you since I can't prove you knew she was underage, but you're walking a thin fucking line."

"I gotchu," he replied nonchalantly. His phone dinged and he looked at it. "I'm gonna step out front for a smoke," he said.

My head turned real quick to glance around the bar and make sure everyone was good on drinks, then said, "I'll step out with you. I could burn one, anyway."

Fletch kinda shrugged as if he didn't want me to follow, but we stepped out onto the front patio. Every time I saw those steps, I thought about Kayla. We stood there in silence for a few minutes, then I said, "You know you got what you deserved, right?"

"Yeah, probably."

"One thing you don't do to a man is fuck his sister behind his back," I said, wincing slightly at my own hypocrisy with Izzy and Clyde. "That'll fuck you up real good."

"Yeah, I guess."

We were quiet for another minute, then I tossed my cigarette. Just as I was about to walk back in, though, a familiar car pulled up in front of the bar.

It was Kayla's.

With a furrowed brow, I shot a puzzled look in her direction. A tinted windshield made it so I could only just barely see her inside the car. "Fucking great," I breathed.

"This is gonna be good." I lit another cigarette and, for a moment, I stood there expecting her to get out of the car – but that didn't happen. Instead, Fletch descended the steps and walked up to the passenger door. "What the fuck…?" I muttered to myself.

"I'll be back in a minute," Fletch said to me. He then got in the car. Kayla looked at me for a brief moment before she drove off. I didn't know what to do as I stood on the porch of the Hole seething, confused, vitriolic and enraged. The cigarette flew from my hand as I flicked it and walked back inside.

What was she doing with Fletch? What kind of fucking drugs did he have her on? I hoped to god it was only for drugs. The thought of her fucking that filthy man made my blood scream to a boil. I could have burned the whole place down right then and there.

"Hey," Izzy said as I walked in, "I'm gonna go over to Clyde's for a bonfire, you wanna go when you get off?"

I said nothing, just stood there staring at the wall.

"You okay?" Izzy asked from her stool, noticing my troubled visage.

"You should leave."

"What? What's wrong?"

"Closing early. I'll text you tomorrow."

She looked at me with worry and confusion, but pulled twenty bucks from her purse and set it on the bar. She got up, touched my arm, and said: "Whatever it is, it'll be okay," then hurried out the door.

I walked back behind the bar, still shaking with anger, turned off the audio system and the bar immediately became quiet. "Hey, what the hell!" somebody yelled.

My voice boomed, "Everybody pay your tabs and go. Bar's closing."

"What the fuck, it's not even eleven-thirty!"

"I still have half a beer left."

"Fuck that, I'll leave when I'm finished."

As they each voiced their grievances, I grabbed a bottle of jack from the bar and drank straight from the bottle for a moment, gulped it down, then in a swift motion shattered it against the bar as glass debris and caustic liquid exploded into the air. That shut everyone the fuck up real quick. I roared, "I said *get the fuck out of my bar!*"

That time they listened. Quickly, they all set cash for their tabs on the bar, except for a few who simply ran out. I didn't care. As soon as they all were out, I grabbed another bottle of some cheap shit whiskey and stepped out the door, planting myself on the steps as I drank. Finally, Kayla's car pulled back up. Without losing a second, I flew down the steps. The passenger door opened and as Fletch went to get out, I grabbed him by the shirt collar and pulled him out myself. "Bar's closed. Go the fuck home, Fletch." My heart pounded so loudly in my eardrums that I couldn't even hear his protesting. Instantly, I sat myself down in the passenger seat.

"West, what the fuck!" Kayla shouted. "Get out of my fucking car!"

"What the fuck are you doing with Fletch?"

"None of your goddamn business. In case you didn't realize this, you're not my fucking boyfriend."

"I don't give a shit, what are you doing with Fletch?"

"West, I swear to god if you don't get out of this fucking car – "

"Call the fucking cops on me, I don't care. Maybe you can tell *them* what you're doing with the biggest fucking drug dealer in town."

"Go fuck yourself, West."

I was absolutely piss hammered by that point, on the verge of blacking out. "You buying coke? Is that where you want your life to go? Just become another worthless Matchstick fucking coke whore?"

"It's none of your fucking business!"

"He give you a discount for a fucking blowie?"

"You're a fucking psycho, West."

"Psycho? You think I'm a psycho?" Spit flew from my mouth as I laughed in her face. "I'm one bad day away from being the top story on fucking CNN, you have no idea how much of a fucking psycho I am."

That might have been the first time I'd ever seen real, genuine fear of me in Kayla's eyes. I didn't like it. "West," she said in a low voice. "Get out of my car."

For a second, I sat there biting my tongue. Finally, I looked at her and said, "If I see you around Fletch again…" Our eyes locked as she shrank back into her seat. I thought about my father's story of the gambler. "I'll fucking kill him. I swear to god I will." With that, I got out of the car and watched her as she sped off. I wanted to do bad things. Violent things. Things that would make God turn his head in horror.

I took another swig from the bottle of whiskey and that's the last thing I remembered.

Chapter 6

Birds chirped their shrill songs as I woke up by the dumpster behind the bar face down in the alley with a malevolent fucking headache. The sun was high in the sky and the birds were singing in the cool breeze, but my mouth felt like a desert and my body like it had been hit by a truck.

"Hey, you alive?" Clyde's voice came from above me. He nudged me roughly with his foot. "Hey, Earth to Weston, wake the fuck up." I could hear him chuckle as I pushed myself up off the ground wearily. The sun blinded me for a moment as I rolled onto my ass and sat up. "Ahh, there it is," Clyde said with a grin from ear to ear. "Rough night?"

"Fucking apparently," I groaned. My tongue was like a roll of fucking sandpaper in my mouth.

Clyde pulled a bottle of water from his backpack and handed it to me. "Here, drink it. You look like shit."

Cool water washed over my parched mouth as I took a drink. "Thanks for pointing that out, great way to start my day."

"Oh trust me, it gets even better," he said with an expression somewhere between mischievous and bracing for impact, like there was some great secret he was privy to that I wasn't.

"What do you mean?"

"Maybe go inside first."

I looked around and realized where I was, just by the seven foot tall fence around the back patio of the Hole.

Clyde had his own set of keys to the place. Sometimes he'd go in early and do some cleaning to cover the spots me or my father missed the night before. Other times he'd go in and just sit and smoke weed and drink by himself on his days off. I took my phone out of my pocket to check the time, but all I got was a blank screen and a dead battery. "What time is it?" I asked as I got to my feet.

"'Bout twelve-thirty. Jim will probably be here soon."

"Fucking great." We walked through the back gate and entered the bar from the back door. What we were met with was a fucking horror show.

Barstools were overturned and strewn about; shelves were broken; bottles of liquor lay scattered about the floor, some broken, some still intact. It was a fucking mess.

"Shit..." I muttered. "I think I might have fucked up."

Clyde finally burst into laughter. "You don't fucking say?"

Without another word, but with a slight groan, I set about picking up the bottles and barstools. Clyde set his backpack down on one of the tables and started to help out. "What got up *your* ass last night?" he asked.

"I don't really remember," I replied, racking my brain for some semblance of recollection. "I blacked out pretty hard."

"Izzy said you closed the bar down at like eleven last night."

"Something like that." It started coming back to me.

"What inspired *that* bold business decision?" Clyde asked.

My chest heaved as I let out a sigh and said, "I think it was Kayla."

"What, did she show up here asking for you to pay for her abortion again?"

Normally, I might have laughed. But there was a heavy guilt sitting on my chest about last night – whether it was from the parts that I remembered or the parts that I didn't, I wasn't sure. "No," I sighed. "She came here to meet Fletch."

"Fletch? What's she want to do with that lowlife piece of shit?"

"I'm not sure. He got into her car and they left for ten or fifteen minutes and came back. When she got back, I jumped in the car and gave her the third degree."

"And?"

Blank. "I don't remember shit. All I know is I was mad and said some things I shouldn't have said. After that I just blacked the fuck out."

"Can't let the bottle be your best friend, West," Clyde said, clicking his tongue. "It'll get you into all kinds of trouble."

My head turned as I looked around the destruction in the bar and said, "Yeah, apparently."

A few minutes later, the front door swung open and my father stepped in. I dreaded his reaction, expecting him to shout, berate me, probably even throw a couple hands at me. Instead he just walked in, shook his head and sighed. "God fucking damn it, West."

"Sorry...." was all I could say. Most of the chaos had been returned to order, but the broken things stayed broken.

Jim walked over to the bar and set his things down. "Fletch called me last night, said you closed the bar in some sort of fit of fury. I figured I'd be walking into an abandoned warzone when I got here, but god damn." He shook his head again.

"Fucking Fletch," I breathed.

"You know this is coming out of your paycheck, don't you?" my father asked.

"Yeah, I figured. That's fair."

"I don't give a fuck if you think it's fair or not," Jim erupted. "Thank you for your consideration, but you're lucky I don't fire your ass." He then looked at Clyde. "Clyde, go home. I'll call you when I'm ready to open up tonight. Let West clean up his own mess."

Clyde shot me a look to say he wanted to remain and help but he wasn't going to cross my father. He shook my hand and said, "Later, bro." As Clyde left, I went into the kitchen behind the bar and plugged my phone into a charger affixed in an outlet on the wall, then went back to work. My father stood there going over bills and order forms as I slowly restored the bar back to its former lack of glory. As I cleaned, my mind went back to Fletch. It felt like I should have fucked him up when I had the chance. Should have pulled him from that car and curb stomped him till his teeth cracked on the pavement. My mind drifted back to one of my earliest memories of the Hole in the Ground, back before my dad bought it. I couldn't have been more than six or seven years old at that point.

We would go to the bar on a regular basis when I was a kid. Dad would get off work and he'd bring me with him to the Hole as a way of saving money from hiring a babysitter. My mom had been dead for a few years by that point – drunk driver took her from us – and I was at my father's side almost constantly.

There was this one night we were in there, me propped up on a barstool so I could play the old arcade machine in the corner, him sitting at the bar carrying on with his friends. Suddenly the laughter turned into angry words and shouting. The memory is so old that I don't remember what exactly was said, but my dad said the guy had called my mom a bitch. They almost went to blows right then and there in the bar, but the bartender reminded Jim that he had his kid with him and that a night in jail would be good for neither of us.

After a while, we left the bar. But instead of driving off, we sat in the truck for several minutes.

"Dad, why aren't we leaving?" I asked.

He anxiously rapped his fingers against the steering wheel, watching the bar door with focus and intent. His breath smelled like an amalgamation of beer and liquor as he spoke. "I've gotta take care of something, West," he said.

"Take care of what?"

Jim thought for a second, then replied, "You saw that man that was in there tonight? The one arguing with me?"

"Yeah."

"He said some bad things about your mother."

"Bad things? What bad things?"

Jim scratched his neck for a moment, then said, "Called her bad names. I can't let that slide. Don't ever let a man disrespect the women in your life, no matter who it is."

I nodded as if I understood but I didn't have a fucking clue what he was talking about. I had barely heard anything that had been said between the two of them. Then, a moment later, the man in question came through the door and down the steps. "Stay here," my father commanded. He opened his door and gripped his keys between his knuckles. I saw his shadowy silhouette walk up to the man, and before any words could be spoken, my father started beating him. My face lit up with fear and surprise. He knocked him to the ground with just a couple of hits, then dropped down onto the man's chest with his knee and pummeled his face into the asphalt. I could only imagine the keys in between my dad's fingers cut the man's face something fierce.

Within seconds, my dad was back in the car and we hurriedly sped off. "Remember, West – what I just did there, it might look bad, but I did the right thing. Don't ever let another man disrespect your woman. It might make me look like a monster, but you need people with the devil in them to take care of the really evil fucks."

As I cleaned the bar, I felt that I should have given the same brutal treatment to Fletch.

***

It was after four when I was finally done cleaning. It was exhausting work. My father had barely spoken a word during the whole ordeal.

"Looks like I can finally open for the fucking night," Jim grumbled.

But as he said that, I stared through the front door with a sinking feeling in my gut. "Yeah, and I think we might have our first customers walking in right now." Parked in front of the bar on the street was a Matchstick Police Department cruiser. Two cops in uniform stepped out and walked up the stairs almost apprehensively, like they knew they weren't welcome. One was darker skinned and one the other was Bill Sparks. Instinctively, I made myself scarce and hid in the kitchen. Bill spoke first.

"Jim," he stated flatly.

"Bill," my father replied equally flatly. They had known each other for over thirty years and as far as I knew, Bill always hated my father. His reasons were beyond me, but he carried a disdain for that man on his shoulders for longer than I had been alive.

"Sorry to bother you," the darker one addressed my father. "My name is Officer Watson. We're looking for Weston Ryder."

Fuck. My heart sank into my bowels. My father spoke. "What's this about?"

"We got a call about a young lady named Kayla Sparks. The person who called it in said Weston is her boyfriend."

Bill stepped in and said, "Sorry, Watson here is new on the force. What he *meant* to say is that I'm looking for my daughter and I've got a bug up my ass telling me that her boyfriend might have a clue as to why."

"*Ex*-boyfriend," I corrected him as I stepped out from the kitchen. Bill looked at me.

"You always hide from the cops or just when you've got a reason?" he asked.

"Maybe I've always got a reason." I held my position firmly, hiding the fact that I was scared shitless. What the fuck did I do last night?

"Do you know anything about Kayla's night last night?" Bill asked me.

My mind flashed back to our argument in her car. "No idea. She came by here for a minute, we talked in her car, and then she drove somewhere else – where that else is I have not a fucking clue, your majesty." Jim shot me a look of disapproval at my snide comment.

The other cop spoke up. "She still drive the white Honda Accord?"

"Yeah," I answered. "Why?"

Bill spoke again. "Because her car is still parked down the street."

"*What?*" I asked, almost startled.

My father spoke next: "What exactly was this call about, officer?"

Officer Sparks sighed and said, "According to her roommate, Kayla never made it home last night. Her friends haven't been able to contact her via her cell phone or social media. Last time anybody contacted her was around one-thirty in the morning. Have you talked to her since last night, Weston?"

"No," I declared. "I was here all night."

"All night as in...?"

"All night as in I woke up here this morning."

Bill eyed me with a puzzled look. "Do you remember going to sleep here, or...?"

"Christ, does anybody remember when they fall asleep?"

The two cops exchanged glances, then Watson asked, "What time did you see Kayla last night?"

"Around eleven-thirty, I believe."

"You believe?"

"Sorry I didn't think to jot this down," I remarked with rude sarcasm. "It was some time between eleven-thirty and midnight."

"And you haven't heard from her at all today?"

"No."

Watson muttered something into his radio, then said, "Well, give us a call if you hear anything. We're canvassing the area to find her, but usually missing persons turn up within a day or so."

"And if they don't?" I asked fearfully.

Bill looked me dead in my eyes like he was giving me a warning shot. "Then that's an entirely different conversation we would be having."

With that, the cops left. My father's watchful eye peered at me as I watched them go. As soon as they were gone, I bolted into the kitchen and powered on my phone. The minute or so it took for it to boot was unbearable. Finally, as it came on, I blitzed through my notifications.

No texts from Kayla, no Facebook messages, no Snapchats. But there was one thing.

I had a missed call from Kayla from around one in the morning. The fear that something terrible had happened was real, but I tried to brush it off, figuring she ended up getting coked out and landed in some guy's apartment.

But just below the missed phone call on the screen was another phone call from Kayla – a video call, according to the record. That time I had apparently answered, though I had absolutely zero recollection of it. The call only lasted a few seconds. What got me, however, was the timing of it.

The cops said the last time someone had gotten ahold of Kayla was around one-thirty in the morning.

Our phone call took place at two twenty-three A.M.

Was I the last person to talk to her?

Chapter 7

I didn't take part in the search for Kayla. Hell, I didn't know if there even *was* one yet. As far as I was concerned, she would turn up when she turned up. The bleeding hearts of Facebook all shared her picture and her circumstances, urging other people to find her just to assuage their own guilt from their armchair detective work, being too unconcerned or too lazy to actually go out and look for her. It felt like a part of us all figured she was just completing her downward spiral.

So I didn't start looking for her yet. Didn't even try to call her. Instead, I did what I did best – went to a bar and got fucking wrecked.

That time it was one of the bars I didn't usually go to, one called the Black Rock Tavern, situated in a little village called Black Rock about fifteen minutes from the Hole. I'd only been there a couple of times. There was a small overlap of the Hole crowd, the Julia's Tavern crowd, and the Black Rock crowd, so I knew a few faces. Fletch was there with his ever struggling girlfriend Kimmy, another regular at the Hole. He probably fucked other women more often than he fucked her and everybody but her seemed to know it. Along with them was a married couple in their forties who also frequented the hole, Dane and Matilda. Matilda had a penchant for young bucks to fuck behind Dane's back, probably the biggest open secret in the entire town – next to Fletch peddling coke, anyway. And then there was Jordan. Jordan hated my fucking guts for reasons I didn't quite understand. His girl had left him a few months ago and she and I ended up at the same bar as him one night. I didn't fuck her, but Jordan didn't seem to know that tidbit of information. He would never actually air any of these issues with me, but he would passive-aggressively make it known by saying things like, "You've got some big fucking shoes to fill." Jordan was an idiot.

Along with all of them was a man I had never met before, except maybe in passing, who introduced himself as Neil. I didn't say more than five words to him, but he was around.

Fletch and Matilda sat on either side of me while I stood between them, with Kimmy on the other side of Fletch and Dane and Jordan off shooting pool. Matilda talked to me. "Haven't seen you in this place for a while," she said, leaning closer to me. "Got tired of the Hole in the Ground?"

I shrugged. "Kinda pissed off my dad," I told her. "I got shit hammered last night and trashed the bar. Besides, I was here a couple weeks ago."

"Is that why they were closed this afternoon?" she asked. "I saw the sign said closed for maintenance."

"Yeah, *I* was the maintenance," I joked half-heartedly.

"That's a shame," Matilda replied sympathetically. She put her hand on my forearm. "I'm sure he'll get over it. Your dad did a good job with you – genetics and everything."

"Thanks," I replied disinterestedly. There was no part in me that was interested in getting tangled with a married woman.

Fletch spoke up. "You hear anything about Kayla yet?" he asked.

"Not a fucking whisper," I replied. "I figured she was with you."

Kimmy shot him a stern look. Fletch shrugged and shook his head. "I didn't talk to her at all after she came by the Hole last night."

Kimmy asked, "What did you talk to her about?" You could tell what she was driving at.

"Just stuff," Fletch said. "Talking about moving to North Carolina, asking about ways to make money down there, that kind of thing. She knows I know some people in Charlotte."

The way he spoke made it clear he wasn't showing his full hand. "The fuck she wanna move to North Carolina for?" I asked suspiciously.

"You'd have to ask her."

Matilda took the proverbial talking stick. "I hope she's okay," she said with feigned worry. Matilda didn't give two shits about Kayla, but her appearance to her friends was paramount. "You guys were so good together."

I laughed audibly. "Sure we were."

Matilda frowned empathetically. "Keep your chin up, West. Handsome guy like you, you'll find someone in no time." She put her hand back on my forearm.

Dear god I wanted to break the uncomfortability but luckily someone else did for me. The bartender Victoria began shouting down at the other side of the bar at a tall man with a scraggly beard. "If I get one more complaint about you making passes at the girls, you're done for the night. No means no," she said sternly, loudly enough for everyone to hear. She then came down to our corner to check our drinks.

Kimmy said, "Someone causing trouble?"

Victoria inhaled sharply and widened her eyes exasperatedly. "This freaking guy keeps fucking creeping on the all the girls and talking about his dick and shit, it's making people uncomfortable."

"So kick him out," I suggested.

"He does it again and I will."

"Fuck that," I blurted. "Guys like that don't get a second chance."

Matilda said, "Can't be too careful with guys like that. I'm pretty sure somebody slipped something into me and Kimmy's drinks a couple weeks ago."

"Really?" I asked in surprise.

"Mhm," Matilda nodded. "We had, what, three or four drinks? And both of us were more fucked up than we had ever been in our lives."

"Jesus Christ," I said.

"Luckily Dane was there and he got us back safe. But still, it's a scary reality we live in."

"Jesus Christ," I repeated. "This is why I don't try new bars."

After a moment, Matilda spoke to me again. "Speaking of trying new places," she said in a forced manner, "have you ever been to the Lamplight diner?"

"Not that I know of," I said.

"I go there all the time, the food is amazing. You should come with me sometime."

Jesus fucking christ. "Sure," I replied nonchalantly.

"What's your number?" she asked. "No, wait – add me on Facebook?"

"Sure," I grunted again. As we became "friends" on the virtual meat market, Dane sauntered over.

"Matilda, you're up," he said, pointing his thumb at the pool table.

She looked at him and said, "Okay," then looked back at me and said, "I'll text you."

As Matilda and Dane went and played pool, Fletch and Kimmy eventually gravitated over to a table along the wall to sit with Jordan and Neil. I was left by myself in the corner of the bar. At some point, the tall man who had been creeping came and stood behind me, trying to get another drink. I could see the Hole people pointing and speaking in low voices as Dane and Matilda joined them. Figured they were talking about the guy behind me, who got kicked out just a few minutes later.

Finally, one o'clock rolled around. The bar crowd had dwindled down to fewer than a dozen people, the sad fucks among us who can go till the daylight comes. I had reached my desired level of intoxication, was just getting ready to pay and fuck off when Neil came up to me.

Before I could say anything, he spoke: "Hey, man," he began. He was older, had dark gray hair that could use a trim, and bore an ironic resemblance to Neil Gaiman. "I'm only gonna tell you this once: the game is up." He had an expression of thorough seriousness and gravity in his voice. I had no fucking clue what he was going on about.

"What the fuck are you talking about?"

He looked around. "There's six, seven people in this bar who want to kick your ass right now. We know what you get up to. Do yourself a favor – pay your tab and leave."

Quickly I glanced around the bar. Couldn't spot anybody I knew who had a real problem with me. Everyone I knew from the Hole had already left. "Dude, what the fuck are you talking about?" I repeated. "I didn't do anything."

"I know what you do," Neil reiterated. "You've been slipping shit into girls' drinks."

The mixture of confusion and rage was indescribable. "I *what*? Where the fuck did you get that idea?"

"Look," Neil went on in a low voice, "there are people from the Hole in the Ground here. They all pointed at *you* specifically. They said 'that guy with the devil tattoo – don't trust that guy.' They said 'we've seen him slipping drugs into girls' drinks when they aren't looking.' So do yourself a favor and go home, and don't come back. You got it?"

"I'm telling you, you're confused, man. You want to fucking frisk me? I don't have fucking roofies."

Neil put his palms up in defense. "Hey, man, when shit goes down don't say nobody warned you. We've got our eyes on you." With that, Neil returned to his table.

Fury coursed through my body as I stood there shaking. What the fuck was he talking about? I wanted to leave – not because some prick told me to, but because I wanted to go to bed – but I stayed and ordered another beer just to show him I didn't give two fucks about his appraisal of me.

I was the last one to leave the bar that night. As I left, I tried to dismiss what happened as a weird one off occurrence. Thought I would go to bed and forget about it.

But I couldn't have been any more wrong.

Chapter 8

Kayla still hadn't turned up the next day. I would be lying if I said that I wasn't starting to become concerned, but I pushed those thoughts from my mind. There was only one objective that afternoon: to find the five Hole regulars who were at Black Rock the night before. Figured the best place to start would be the Hole.

I strolled in at four-thirty. Jane was working the bar. Fletch and Dane sat beside each other.

"Hey, West," Jane said. "You're here early. What, some Tinder date blew you off?"

"Bitch, you *wish* you could blow me off," I joked back playfully.

Jane chuckled. "Jack and coke?"

"Skip the coke and just give me a shot of jack, I won't be here long."

"Healthy choices," Jane joked.

I walked down over to Fletch and Dane as Jane poured me the shot. "Hey," I greeted.

"What's up," Dane replied flatly, not looking up from his phone.

"You guys happen to hear any weird rumors about me last night?"

Fletch looked up. "Weird rumors like what?"

"Like that I slip shit into girls' drinks so I can rape them."

Dane and Fletch exchanged glances. Fletch replied, "Not that I remember. I don't think anybody was really talking about you. I mean, we talked about Kayla a little bit but I don't think anybody called you a rapist. That's kinda wild."

"Why?" Dane asked. "Something happen after we left last night?"

I shook my head. "Just this fucking guy," I muttered. Jane handed me the shot and I downed it. Shit barely even burned anymore I was so used to it, I realized as I took a ten out of my wallet and placed it on the bar. "You know where Jordan's hanging out today? Or Kimmy?"

"Kim's at work all day," Fletch said. "Jordan's probably shooting pool at Julia's Tavern."

"Got it, thanks," I said, then walked out and lit a cigarette as I stood on the steps of the bar, looking around the scenery through my dark sunglasses in the brilliant afternoon sunlight. Matchstick had all of the vibes of a small town, like it was ripped straight from a book. Small shops dedicated to its history as a railroad station littered the place. There was even a defunct train planted right across the street from the bar as some sort of half-assed tourist attraction, along with a railway themed cafe. I was constantly torn between loving the place and fucking detesting it. There was something to be said for community, but I didn't know what it was. In a place where everybody knows everybody, you couldn't really be a nobody. I didn't know if that was good or bad, all I knew is I wanted to get away from it. Questions had started to creep in, like how many of my friends were really in my corner, how many I could really trust, and how many were really just waiting for me to let my guard down so they could pounce. I'd fucked and fought my way into the ill graces of a lot of people. There was no shortage of Matchstick residents who had a bone to pick with me.

The next stop was Julia's Tavern. Jordan was there shooting pool just like Fletch had said, so I got a beer from Paul and sauntered over to the pool room. Jordan was practicing his shots by himself. "Hey," I said.

"What's good, West," Jordan replied disinterestedly as he lined up a shot.

"I've got a couple of questions about last night."

"I'm kind of in the middle of something right now."

"Shooting by yourself?"

"It's called practice."

I thought for a moment and said, "Rack it up, I'll play you."

Jordan looked at me then shrugged, momentarily putting his disdain for me to the side. "Sure."

As he racked the balls, I eased into the questions. I knew Jordan wouldn't hesitate to be a pain in the ass. He knew something I didn't, and he knew that I wanted to know. I'd have to play an angle to get anything out of him.

"You break," I said. Jordan lined up his shot with the cue ball and slammed it into the tight triangle formation of the rest of the balls, sending them scattering. "You know that guy, Neil? The one from last night?"

"Not really," Jordan replied, setting up another shot. "I hadn't ever seen him before last night. He doesn't normally go to bars, I don't think."

"He doesn't seem to like me very much." Jordan sank a few more balls, then finally left the table open for me.

The pool stick rested on my fingers and I propped up my arm for a shot. "Said some pretty enlightening shit last night," I said as I sank one of my balls. "You know anything about that?"

"Enlightening shit like what?" Jordan asked as I pocketed another one.

"Said he'd heard things about me from the Hole regulars. Some pretty vile shit." I kept what I knew close to the vest to see if Jordan would offer that information voluntarily, slip up and admit that he knew damn well what I was talking about. Deliberately, I missed my next shot.

It gave Jordan a good leave, setting him up to run the table for the next couple of turns. "Can't imagine why," he said with a hint of sarcasm. "People saying bad things about *you*? What a shocking turn of events." He hit every shot he took until it came down to the eight ball and he couldn't quite sink it.

"I've never met the guy," I replied as I cleared the rest of my balls. "He said he'd heard things from one of you." The table lined up for the perfect shot at the eight ball. Figured if I sank it, Jordan would shut down the line of communication. Carefully, I lined up my shot so I would just barely miss the eight ball.

Jordan grinned and stepped back to the table, lined up the shot and sank the eight ball effortlessly. He wore his pride in the victory clearly on his face. "Good game," he sneered. "But hey, if you're not putting shit into anyone's drinks then you've got nothing to worry about, right?"

There it was. "You know who started that line of thinking?" I asked as I shook his hand and set down my pool stick.

"No idea," Jordan said. I was inclined to believe him. "All I'm gonna say is you better hope Kayla turns up soon."

"Why?" I asked.

"'Cause if she doesn't, you're gonna have a lot of people coming after you. Cheers." He toasted me with his drink.

***

Izzy stayed with me that night. She came over with a handle of Captain and a case of soda for a night of debauchery and movies. "God it's been a fucked up day," I said as she wrapped her arms around me.

"You figure out who was spreading those rumors yet?"

"No," I shook my head. "I'm still hoping it was a case of mistaken identity, but right now all I want to do is drink and forget."

"You're not already drunk?" she teased.

"I didn't say that," I grinned devilishly. "It's the forgetting part that I need help with."

"Well then, allow me." Izzy pressed her lips against mine. I'm sure she could taste the rum soaked into them. She pulled away after a second and I took a gulp straight from the handle.

An hour later and I was heading back into blackout territory.

Izzy sat on top of me on my couch, her dress draped over my legs as she moved up and down, exhaling with excited pleasure. My fingers ran through her hair and pulled her closer with my other hand firmly holding her ass. Heaven would have been that moment lasting forever: every sound of her voice as she took a breath and let out a moan; every gyration of her hips as she rocked my body with hers; the sensation of our bodies becoming one until we both came in a fit of ecstasy.

She rested her chin on my shoulder as she sat on top of me panting and catching her breath and holding each other tightly. Something came over me. I whispered into her ear, "You don't have to say anything, and I'm sorry if this is too soon or it catches you off guard. But I think I'm in love with you. Everything in my world is better for having you in it. You are my best friend and I never want that to change. I really, truly, deeply love you."

After that everything went black again.

At eight o'clock in the morning, Izzy woke me up. "Hey, sleeping beauty," she said sweetly. "I gotta get to work."

My stomach and my head hurt so fucking bad that death would have been preferable to living. "Urkay," I groaned, "have fun." I felt like I caught a look of concern on her face but I passed out again before I could process it. Then, a moment later, it was four in the afternoon and Izzy was crawling back into my bed.

"Hey," she said, shaking me. "You alive?"

After twelve hours of sleeping, I was awake – with a hangover so fucking fierce it could have been the one that finally killed me. "Fucking barely," I groaned. Izzy laid down next to me and put her leg over my midsection.

"Ready for another round?" I asked, despite the fact that I could barely move.

"You desperately need a shower and a breath mint, so no," Izzy chuckled faintly. "And you have to be at work in an hour, so... chop chop."

"Ugh, fucking kill me," I groaned. Suddenly, I felt a vibration on the side of my leg. After a moment it finally registered that my phone was ringing. It was Jane. "Hey, what's up?" I asked wearily.

"*Hey, weird question. Did you get arrested?*"

"I mean yeah, a couple of times."

"*No, I mean like recently.*"

"How recently?"

"*Like last night recently.*"

I furrowed my brow and looked at Izzy. "Not that I can recall," I said. "I think I've got a pretty solid alibi for last night."

"*So you weren't arrested for raping someone last night?*"

Eyebrows raised. "Pretty sure the sex I had last night was consensual, unless you wanna ask her." Izzy smacked me on the shoulder.

"*That's what I figured. Somebody called here a little bit ago and said you were arrested in Antioch for rape and all kinds of shit.*"

My chest rose and fell as I let out a sigh. "Who called and said that?"

"*It was a cop.*"

I sat upright immediately. "What?" I asked.

"*Just get over here, it'd be easier to explain it all in person.*"

"Fucking great," I muttered. "Alright, I'll be there soon." Disconnected.

"What was that all about?" Izzy asked.

"I'm not sure yet," I replied, staring at my phone screen. "But I think someone is after me."

Chapter 9

Rumors spread like wildfire. Somehow, it seemed like I was the last person to know about these phone calls.

Bracing myself, I walked through the door of the Hole to find the usual crowd. The air became palpably uncomfortable as people turned and looked at me. Wasting no time, I immediately walked up to Jane, who was bartending along with my father. I looked at my dad and asked, "What are you doing here? I didn't think you worked today."

"I didn't," he began, "but I think you might need the night off."

"What?" I asked. "What for?"

Jane spoke. "We weren't the only bar to get a phone call," she said.

My eyes narrowed. "Which other places did they call?"

Jane frowned and said, "All of them."

"*All of them?*" I repeated.

Jane nodded. "Julia's, Black Rock, even the Station."

"I barely ever even go to the fucking station," I protested. "It's like a fucking retirement home in there."

"Yeah, I know that," Jane replied. "But I don't think people care if you go there or not."

"Fuck me...." I muttered. "Tell me about the phone call."

"So this guy calls and says he's a cop with the Coal County Sheriff's Department – "

"Wow, we jumped right over the MPD's head, didn't we?" I interrupted.

" – and he said, 'Does Weston Ryder ever go to your bar?' And I said, 'Yeah, why?' And he's like, 'Last night, Mr. Ryder was arrested for drugging girls at a bar in Antioch, rape and attempted rape, kidnapping, and assault.' I asked which bar and he said he couldn't give me that information, but he was calling all of the bars in the area to let them know."

My father looked at me suspiciously and said, "None of that is true, is it?"

"The fuck do you think?" I shot back.

"Where were you last night?" my father then asked. "When people start asking questions – and believe me, they'll be asking questions – the only thing that'll help you is if you've got somewhere you can provably have been."

My gut tightened. Clyde still didn't know about me and his sister. What a fucking spot to be in. My voice came out in a low whisper, practically drowned out by the bar music, "Don't tell Clyde, but I was with Izzy all night. We were at my place."

Jane and my father exchanged surprised looks. Jane said, "Seriously? You're hooking up with Izzy?"

"Yeah," I replied with a grimace. "So at the very least, she can vouch for me. What else did the cop say?"

Jane shrugged. "Nothing, really."

"Are you sure it was actually a cop?" I asked.

"It sounded pretty legit," Jane explained. "The words and terms he used, the way he spoke – it definitely seemed like he knew what he was talking about."

"You think maybe it was Bill?" I asked.

"That was kind of my first thought, but he said he was from the Sheriff's department and Bill is with Matchstick."

"That's true," I said, "but maybe he was covering his trail. Did anybody else from the Sheriff's department or anything call you?"

"No."

"Can you call them back?"

A lightbulb went off in Jane's head. "That's actually a pretty good idea."

"You say that as if I don't normally have good ideas."

My dad chimed in. "Because you fucking don't."

Jane grabbed the phone docked by the cash register and went back through the call history until she found the one from earlier. She redialed the number and held the handset up to her ear for a moment. But as the dial tone ceased, her face fell into one of surprise and puzzlement.

"What is it?" I asked.

"That's weird…" she said airily. "Why don't you try calling it? I don't know if I'm hearing this right."

Wordlessly, she handed me the phone, so I called the number and I put it to my ear.

"The TextNow subscriber you are trying to reach has disconnected their service. We're sorry."

Click.

As the line disconnected, I looked up with wide eyes at Jane and handed back the phone. "What the fuck…?"

***

There was work to do that evening. Jane had said every other bar in town – and the collective vicinity – had received a similar phone call. I knew this had to have something to do with Kayla, but for the fucking life of me I couldn't figure out what.

But I needed answers.

First stop was Julia's Tavern. I was tense as I stepped through the doors. Within a second, I could feel everybody's eyes on me. They all knew who I was – whether or not they did the day before, they all knew who I was now. Paul saw me and immediately went into the back – presumably to start calling people and tell them where to find me.

Jack, a former bouncer at the Hole, was sitting at the bar as I approached it. He saw me and leapt to his feet. "West, I'm gonna have to ask you to leave," he said. Jack was a tough guy in his mid-forties. He used to tangle with trouble like it was no problem but a couple of knee injuries put him out of the game. Ex-military, private security, that type of thing. And even with a bad knee he could snap me like a fucking twig. "We don't want any trouble." He placed his hand on my shoulder and squeezed it.

"I'll go, I'll go," I said with my palms up but my eyes narrowed and my stance remained solid. "But I've got a few questions first."

Jack looked back over his shoulder at Paul as he created a barrier between me and the bar. Paul held a phone in his hand, not having dialed anybody yet. He came over. "Look, West," he began, "I don't know what's going on, but we got a very concerning phone call this morning and whatever you're wrapped up in, we don't want any part of it. You're not welcome in this bar."

"I understand that," I said, "and I will leave peacefully. But I just want to ask – did you check my arrest record?"

"What?" Paul replied as he cocked his head.

"If I was arrested, then there should be documentation for that, right? I mean, that's publicly accessible information."

Jack spoke up. "They might not have posted it yet."

"That's true," I went on, "but why don't you go ahead and call the cops back and ask *them*?"

Paul gave Jack a look. "I mean, I have the number written down."

Jack nodded and said, "Go ahead and do that, I'll wait here." Paul disappeared into the back and I stood there as Jack still held me by the shoulder. People looked at me with malice in their eyes, as though I was a walking villain in their stories. I had never wanted a drink so fucking badly in my entire life.

After a minute, Paul came back, looking even more quizzical than before. I said, "Well?"

Paul said, "I got some sort of answering message saying it was a number for some app called TextNow…?"

Jack looked at me, mirroring Paul's confusion. Then I said, "Why don't you call the actual police – MPD or the Sheriff's department – and ask them about it."

Jack nodded to Paul and said, "West, go on and jot down your phone number, Paul will call you as soon as we hear back from the police."

I did as he asked and handed the number to Paul. Jack still hadn't let go of me. "Can I get a drink while I wait?"

Jack shook his head. "No," he said. "You still have to go. It's nothing personal, it's just protection."

"These people don't need protected from me," I assured him.

"No, it's about protection for *you*." Every face was turned on me. Jack leaned in and whispered, "If I walk away, you're not gonna make it out of here alive." I'd like to think he was exaggerating, but I'm not a betting man and that was one hell of a gamble.

As Jack walked me out of the pub, he said, "I'm gonna give you the benefit of the doubt right now. But if I find out this is actually true…" he paused. "I'll beat the fuck out of you myself."

"As you should," I replied before getting into my car.

I repeated the incident at Black Rock right afterward. They, too, were reluctant at first, but after they called the number back, they knew something was up. Before I left, I asked Victoria, "Do you know that guy that was here the other night? Neil, I think his name was?"

"No, not really," she said. "He's only ever been here a couple of times. I'm not sure who his friends are or what his last name is. Why?"

I scoffed and said, "I think he's the one who made the phone calls."

Victoria grimaced sympathetically and said, "I wish I could help but I don't know anything about the guy."

As it stood, though, the Hole in the Ground was the only place in town that wouldn't immediately throw me out. So I went back there. Kimmy sat at the bar and I stood a few feet away from her.

"As soon as I heard that," Kimmy said, "I knew it wasn't true. I even looked at Jane and said, 'West? Really? I don't think he's the kind of guy who would do that.'"

"Well thanks for the vote of confidence," I replied cheerlessly. It was almost like I could feel the eyes on the back of my head. Whether they would admit it or not, everybody except for Jane, Izzy, Clyde, and my father thought I was guilty. Deep down – hell, probably not even that deep – they thought it was true.

Jane must have noticed how forlorn I looked as the night came to a close. She came over to me at the bar and said, "Hey, I'll buy you a drink if you take the trash out for me."

"You're a big girl, you can do it yourself."

"It's not that I can't, it's that I don't want to," she replied with an innocent laugh. "That dumpster in the summertime is absolutely fucking foul."

I laughed and said, "Yeah, that's fair. Alright, make it two drinks and you've got a deal."

"Bet," she said and shook my hand. Drunkenly, I rose to my feet and rounded the bar, grabbed the trash can from its resting place beside the cooler, and picked up the heavy bin of broken bottles to carry it out the back door and through the gate.

The dumpster was right next to where I had woken up the other day, the morning after Kayla went missing. I thought about that and wondered what she would say if she knew the predicament I found myself in. For the first time since she went missing, I found myself actively hoping she was okay. I missed her. It hurt like hell to admit it, but I missed her. I told myself I would apologize for how I'd been the last few days whenever she came back from the bender she was probably on. Told myself maybe we could patch things up – if not as lovers, then as friends.

As I carried the bag of trash over to the dumpster, the smell became suffocating. It was like someone had stuffed my face in roadkill, that sickly scent of rot and decay in the summer heat.

When I opened the lid of the dumpster, it was like a wave of sickness washed over me, the smell was so powerful. Uncontrollably I coughed and gagged, held my hand over my face and dropped the trash bag. Out of morbid curiosity, I switched on my phone's flashlight to see what the hell was in that dump. I moved a few bags out of the way.

Nothing could have prepared me for the horror.

I let out a cry of deep pain so visceral and feral that the sound alone could have peeled the bark from a tree. I roared and I cried as I collapsed to my knees and the world spun around me in the darkness.

Inside of the dumpster beneath the trash was a dead body, sallowed, decayed and bloating in the heat.

It was Kayla.

Chapter 10

Kayla lay next to me as I ran my fingers through her hair. We had been dating for about three months at that point and I was head over heels. We shared a passionate kiss full of love and lust and I stared into her eyes.

"What?" she smiled and hid her face a little.

"Nothing," I replied. "Just…you."

"Yeah?" she said softly. "What about me?"

"I don't think I've ever been this happy before in my life. I'm so glad you found me."

"What can I say, I have a thing for strays," she grinned.

I laughed softly. "I know it's soon, I know we said we should take things slow, but I can't help the way I feel."

"The way you feel?" she asked.

"About you."

"How do you feel about me?"

"I think I'm in love with you." I should have been afraid of how she would respond, but I wasn't. I knew how she felt. And as she pulled me closer and buried her face in my neck, she whispered:

"I think I'm in love with you, too."

That was all over now. Blue and red lights flashed all around me and danced off the walls of the buildings as the crime scene people pulled Kayla's body out of the dumpster. I couldn't look while they did it. I just stared at the ground. Every cop in Matchstick might have been there. Sirens blared as more approached but they all sounded so distant to me. Everything was distant. I sat there catatonically, sitting in the grass with my arms resting on my knees as I slowly dragged on a cigarette to calm my shot nerves.

There are points in a person's life where they know there's no going back. No matter how hard you try, how badly you want, you can never go back to a point before that event. One of those events was finding Kayla at the bar and falling in love. Another was finding Kayla in the dumpster.

She was gone. Nothing would ever fix that.

Bill was inconsolable. They tried to keep him from the scene but he pushed through with brute force. "Where's my fucking daughter?!" he cried. "Where is she?!" Then he saw her. You don't know what pain looks like until you've seen a grown man break. He roared his pain and fury into the night as I sat there in the grass, tears quietly rolling down my cheek. He saw me. "You piece of fucking shit, what did you do to her?!" he screamed.

I said nothing.

Bill lunged at me but Officer Watson and a few others held him back and subdued him, eventually coaxing him into a car and taking him away. A man should never outlive his daughter. It's the cruelest joke the devil ever pulled.

Watson came up to me and sat down in the grass beside me. "How are you holding up, West?" he asked.

I gave him nothing in return.

Watson sighed. "I'm sorry you have to go through this," he said. "But right now we need all of the information we can get. Would you be willing to come back to the station for an interview tonight?"

"An interview or an interrogation?" I asked.

"An interview. You're not being arrested at this time."

At this time, he said. I sighed and said, "Yeah. Yeah, I can do that."

Watson placed his hand on my shoulder for a moment then rose to his feet and went back over to the other police officers. The crime scene people were excavating the dumpster looking for anything that might resemble a clue. Clyde's car pulled up right outside the police line – an old Cadillac that he considered his pride and joy – and he and Izzy stepped out.

"Sir," one of the cops said, holding his hand up to stop them, "I can't allow anyone beyond this point."

"Fuck that," Clyde argued, "I work here and that's my friend over there. Let me fucking talk to him." Izzy looked over at me with a deep sadness. She hadn't spoken to me since the other night when I drunkenly told her I loved her.

"Sir, I'm not going to tell you again."

I got up and went over to them. "Stand down, Chief Wiggum," I said unenthusiastically. I ducked under the crime scene tape and wrapped my arms around Izzy. We stood there for a moment as she comforted me. "She's gone, Izzy. She's really gone."

Clyde put his hand on my shoulder. I sensed that he wanted to say something, but I don't think the English language was capable of providing any words for comfort. "We're all in this together, man," was all Clyde could say.

Finally I let go of Izzy. "They're taking me to the police station in a little bit."

Izzy asked, "They're not arresting you, are they?"

"Not yet," I replied. "But if some pretty hard fucking evidence doesn't turn up soon, I don't see any way for this to not be pinned on me."

Izzy frowned wryly and said, "It'll be okay, West."

Watson came over and asked, "You ready to go, West?"

I nodded. He led me to his cruiser and I got in the passenger seat. The drive there was quiet. I had nothing to say.

The MPD station was a relatively small building. It was far from my first time there, but I would have given anything to have been there on vandalism or DUI charges again. Watson brought me in, had me sign some papers, then led me to a small room with a metal table and a few chairs. "You need anything? Coffee, water, food?"

"I'm alright," I said quietly.

Watson nodded and said, "The detective will be with you shortly, alright?"

I nodded back and then Watson left me in the room by myself. It felt like half an hour went by before the door opened again. An older man with a gray beard stepped in. "Weston Ryder?" he asked.

"Unfortunately," I replied.

He held out his hand to shake mine. I didn't take it. The man grimaced and sat down, then said, "My name is Detective Ward. I'm a homicide detective with the Coal County Sheriff's Department. Matchstick doesn't have a dedicated homicide unit, so I'll be working on Kayla's case. Is there anything I can get you?"

"No, thanks."

"In that case, why don't you go ahead and start by telling me about the last time you talked with Kayla."

"It was a couple days ago. She came to the Hole in the Ground – the bar I work at – and talked with a guy named Fletch about things I know not. I confronted her about it – he's a small time dealer – and things got a little heated. But after I got out of her car, she drove off and I never saw her again."

"What kind of things did you talk about?"

"I don't really remember," I admitted. "I asked her what she was doing with Fletch and told her to stay away from him."

"Do you think Fletch would have any reason to want to harm her?"

"Not a fucking clue," I replied callously.

"Is there anyone you can think of who might have a reason to kill her?"

"If I knew that, then I'd be talking to them instead of you."

"Fair enough. Tell me how you found the body."

"I was taking out the trash and the smell coming from the dumpster just wasn't right."

"By the looks of it, she was in that dumpster for a few days. Are you the only one who takes out the trash at the Hole in the Ground?"

"No," I replied, "but usually when the dumpster gets that summer smell, we'll just chuck the bags in as quickly as possible. I don't know how familiar you are with dumpsters, but people don't normally look too closely at them."

"Who else might have taken out the trash in the last few days?"

"Idunno," I shrugged. "Me, Jane, my dad, Clyde maybe. Like I said, we normally do it as fast as we can and get away from there. I'm not surprised nobody found her."

"It's a pretty good hiding spot for a body, isn't it?"

"The fuck kind of question is that?"

"Just an observation." Detective Ward sifted through his notes and said, "I'm gonna level with you, West. It doesn't look good for you. You get into a fight with a woman who broke your heart, she disappears, then you happen to find her body in the dumpster behind your own bar?"

"You saying I did it?"

"No, I'm not saying that. I'm saying it sure looks like someone wants us to think you did it. Any reason somebody might want to get revenge on you, specifically? Any enemies? Anything worth noting?"

"There's definitely something," I offered. "There's been a rumor going around town that I like to roofie girls so I can take them home and date rape them."

"Rumors? How did these rumors start?"

"Still working on that one."

"You think you're being set up?"

"It's looking pretty fucking likely right now, isn't it?"

"Part of my job is to not jump to conclusions. Tempting though it may be, without some names and motives I can't really tie anybody else to this."

"What are you saying?" I asked defensively. "Anybody *else*? Am I a suspect, detective?"

"Not a suspect, not yet. Consider yourself a person of interest."

"Well then," I said as I rose to my feet. The metal chair scraped loudly against the floor. "This person of interest is ending the interview, and the next time you want to talk to me, it'll be with a lawyer present."

"Fair enough," Detective Ward replied. "Before you go, is there anyone or anything at all that's happened recently to Kayla that might be significant? Any new enemies? Bad blood?"

I thought for a moment, then said, "She was robbed leaving the Hole a month or two ago. Maybe whoever did that knows something."

"Did she file a police report?"

"She told me she did. I don't know if they ever followed up, but she reported it."

Ward rose to his feet and said, "I'll check that out. Thanks for coming in, West. If anything else comes to you, please, don't hesitate to give us a call."

As I walked out of the police station, Izzy and Clyde waited for me in Clyde's car. "Well?" Clyde asked.

"They don't know shit," I reported. "From where I'm sitting, it looks like a far cry that the cops will solve this one. They think that I did it."

"They said that?" Izzy asked with concern.

"Not outright but he made it clear enough."

Clyde said, "Where does that leave us?"

Everything that had happened over the last few weeks ran through my mind. "I think we're on our own. And if we don't find out who killed her – " I choked on my words, still unable to accept the reality they represented. "If we don't find who did it, then I'm going down for this."

"Fuck me," Izzy said exasperatedly. "Where do we even start?" My mind immediately jumped to Fletch.

"I think I've got an idea."

Chapter 11

I couldn't sleep that night. How are you supposed to sleep when the person you loved is taken from you? How do you sleep ever again? In lieu of sleeping, I drank myself into a stupor and allowed the memories to assail me while I bit back tears. Every laugh, every kiss, every time we made love – none of it was ever coming back. I remembered when my father met Kayla for the first time.

"Dad, this is Kayla," I introduced him to her on a slow afternoon at the bar as I got there to work.

Jim smiled and shook Kayla's hand. "West won't shut up about you, so you must be doing something right," he said with a smile.

Kayla laughed and replied, "Well, I certainly hope so."

"I've only got one question for you, Kayla: What do you want to do with your life?"

Kayla didn't even have to think about it. "I'm finishing my degree in computer science. I want to open my own business doing work for cryptocurrency companies. If I get in on the ground floor, a couple of small investments could be worth millions in ten years."

My father raised his eyebrows, taken aback. "Wow, that's a good answer. Better than what I've done with my life, that's for damn sure. All I've got to my name is this bar. You're a sharp girl. Keep it up."

Kayla smiled and thanked him, then turned to me and said, "I've gotta get to class, I'll text you later." She kissed me and walked out the door. Jim and I watched her as she left. She had an ass that could make a grown man cry.

My father said, "Don't fuck this one up, West. She's too good for you."

I chuckled and said, "I know that, I just hope that *she* doesn't know that."

Finally, as the memories replayed themselves, I got a couple hours of sleep. I woke up still drunk with a text from Izzy saying she and Clyde were waiting outside for me. Hurriedly, I showered and brushed my teeth, downed a little something, lit up a cigarette and stepped out into the bright early afternoon.

"You holding up?" Clyde asked me as I got into the back of the car. Sunglasses hid my weary eyes.

"As much as I can be," I stated. "Let's do this."

Izzy didn't say anything. She had been distant ever since I slipped up and drunkenly told her that I loved her. I reminded myself that I would have to address that soon. There was a small bouquet of roses – maybe three or four flowers but it was all the store had – tucked back in my apartment that I bought as an apology to Izzy, and still hadn't found the right time to give them to her.

We canvassed all the bars that were open, all of Fletch's usual hangout spots, and turned up nothing. He had made himself scarce, apparently.

Fletch was a surprisingly hard man to find. He had no presence on social media and used a burner phone most of the time. You had to be in his circle to know how to reach him.

I drank from a flask as I sat in the back of the car. "If Fletch knows anything about this, then we're gonna have a hard time tracking him down."

Clyde said, "He's probably holing up in a basement or a bomb shelter somewhere waiting for this to blow over."

"Then let's go knocking on some doors." I wanted payback. I wanted revenge. I wanted to watch the life slowly leak from the eyes of the man who took Kayla from me. I wanted to watch them burn.

Izzy protested. "We can't just go around asking everybody, we'll never find him that way."

"What do you suggest, then, o-wise one?" Clyde asked.

"I bet we can get Kimmy to tell us where he is."

I asked, "So how do we get to Kimmy?"

"The easy way," Izzy replied. She pulled out her phone and dialed Kimmy's number. After a few seconds, Kimmy answered. Izzy said in a friendly voice, "Hey girl, what're you doing?" Kimmy said something back. Izzy replied, "Wanna meet me for lunch? In about half an hour. Yeah, that works. Alright girl, see you soon." She disconnected the call and turned back to look at me. "See? The easy way."

We met Kimmy at a restaurant called Ray's half an hour later. It was a decently nice place with serviceable food and fair prices for drinks. Kimmy was already there waiting for Izzy when we arrived, but she didn't expect me and Clyde. She almost got up to leave when she saw us all approach, but Clyde jumped into the booth and sat beside her before she could get up.

"Surprise," he said.

"What the hell, Izzy?" Kimmy blurted. "I thought it was going to be just us?"

"Yeah, I lied," Izzy dismissed as she sat across from Kimmy.

I sat down next to Izzy. "We aren't here to cause trouble, Kim. We just want to know where Fletch is."

"Why would I tell you that?" Kimmy asked defensively. "Why would anybody trust *you* for anything?"

"Because I didn't kill Kayla," I replied. "And I think your boyfriend might know who did."

"Oh yeah?" Kimmy challenged fearlessly. "How much about the night she died do you remember, West?"

I recoiled. She was right – I didn't remember anything. "Nothing," I admitted. "That's why we need your help."

"Why would I help you?"

"Because if Fletch has anything to do with this – or knows who did – he's gonna have a target on his back."

Kimmy receded slightly and took my words into consideration. "Fletch has nothing to do with this."

Clyde spoke up. "If you really believe that, then there's no harm in us having a little chat with him."

"I don't think that's a good idea," Kimmy rebutted. "He's hiding from someone. I don't know who and I don't know why, but Fletch is scared."

Clyde said to Kimmy, "That means somebody knows something, and eventually everyone else will, too. In a small town like this, how many secrets can you really keep?" Kimmy shot me a glance as I shifted uncomfortably in my seat. Did she know about me and Izzy?

Kimmy spoke. "You'd be fucking surprised."

I said to Kimmy, "If Fletch had anything to do with this, sooner or later somebody *will* find out. And the longer he hides it, the worse it will be for him and everyone else."

Kimmy sighed and finally came around. "I don't know where Fletch is, okay? He said he would be laying low for a few days, told me he'd contact me first."

Clyde said, "Well somebody's gotta know where he is."

Kimmy pressed her finger against her lip as if she just remembered something but wasn't sure she could share it. Izzy asked, "What is it, Kimmy? Does someone come to mind?"

After a moment, Kimmy replied: "I think there actually is somebody he told."

"Who?" I asked.

"Jordan."

Fucking great. Clyde asked, "Where is he right now?"

"If his schedule is still the same, he should be at his workshop right now – the one he does car work out of."

With that, Izzy, Clyde and I all got out of the booth. As we went to leave, Kimmy called out, "Hey, West."

I turned back. "Yeah?"

"You know everyone thinks you did it, right? I mean, from where I'm sitting, it doesn't look like anybody else could have done it. You didn't do it, did you?" There was fear in her voice.

"What do you think?" I asked.

Kimmy shook her head and said, "That's the thing, West. I don't know."

***

Izzy pulled the car into the small gravel parking lot at Jordan's workshop. Jordan was situated underneath a truck he was working on inside of the garage. Clyde turned to Izzy. "Stay in the car."

"What?" she protested. "Why?"

I answered. "Trust us, Tinker Bell. You're gonna want to sit this one out. This could get ugly." Clyde and I exchanged knowing glances. If Jordan didn't want to talk… Well, there's more than one way to persuade a man.

Clyde and I got out of the car and approached Jordan, still lying on a wheel board underneath the truck. Music played loudly in the background. "Hey, Jordan!" Clyde called out.

Jordan slid out from under the truck, took one look at us, then returned to where he was. "Fuck off," he said.

I clicked my tongue and said, "Can't really do that, Jordan. You know why we're here."

"Because you don't have a fucking life?" Jordan retorted.

Clyde said, "We're looking for Fletch. Kimmy doesn't know where he is, but she thinks you might."

"Well," Jordan replied with no concern, "that's because Kimmy's a dumb bitch who can't tell a thumbtack from a thumb in her ass."

"That may be true," I said, "but you're one of the only people Fletch trusts."

"Exactly," Jordan replied from under the truck. "So why would I break that trust by telling you where to find him?"

I said, "Because we're dealing with a dead girl. This isn't some petty drama shit."

Jordan was silent for a moment. "You're gonna need to give me a better reason than that." His legs bent at an angle to push himself forward a little bit. Clyde looked at Jordan's knees, then glanced back at Izzy in the car. She was watching us. Subtly, Clyde motioned for her to turn around. He didn't want her to see what was going to happen next.

Without wasting another breath, Clyde grabbed a crowbar off of a workbench and said, "You need a better reason? I'll give you two," then swung the crowbar into one of Jordan's knees. Jordan cried out in pain. Quickly, I grabbed him and pulled him out from under the truck. Clyde and I lifted him off the ground and threw him onto the hood of the vehicle. "You like that?" Clyde barked.

"What the fuck, man?!" Jordan cried out in pain. I took the crowbar from Clyde and struck Jordan across the face – not hard enough to break anything, but hard enough for it to fucking hurt. I didn't care if it was torture. I needed answers.

"Tell us where the fuck Fletch is," I demanded. "Or the next one is *really* gonna hurt."

Jordan cried out, "He'll fucking kill me if I tell you!"

I said, "Alright, well, ask yourself this – do you want to die later or do you wanna fucking die right now? 'Cause the way I see it, those are about your only options." I didn't know if I would actually kill him, but the rage burning inside me said that I might.

After a moment, Jordan cried out, "Fuck! Alright! Alright! Meet me at the Hole tonight, I'll take you to him."

"Atta boy," I said as Clyde and I released him. Jordan fell to the ground, unable to stand on his knee. "Put some ice on that. Be at the Hole by ten."

As we got back into the car, I thought about what I had done. Gently, my hand brushed against the devil tattoo on my shoulder.

Looking back at Jordan, bruised and weary as we drove off, I remembered what the old woman had called me.

Chapter 12

Clyde and Izzy sat on either side of me at the Hole. They weren't drinking but I was. If I went more than a couple hours without a drink my hands started to shake and my head would hurt. The way I saw it, it was medicine.

Kimmy sat down at the other end of the bar staring at us. Izzy said, almost fearfully, "You guys sure Jordan will show up?" It was nine forty-five.

"He fucking better," I replied.

"Don't worry, he'll show up," Clyde said. Kimmy waved Clyde down over to her end of the bar. Clyde sighed and said, "I'll be right back."

I watched him as he went down and took a seat beside Kimmy. Once he was out of earshot, I turned to Izzy and said, "Hey, can we talk about the other night?"

"You mean when – ?"

"Yeah, when I said that I loved you." I scratched the back of my neck. "I'm sorry, I was drunk and obviously going through some shit. I didn't mean to put that kind of pressure on you. But you've seemed distant since that. So I just wanted to say I'm sorry, and no, I don't love you."

Izzy's face fell. I thought I had said the right thing but now she seemed more upset than before. "Oh," she said flatly. "Gotcha."

I furrowed my brow. "What's wrong? I thought that's what's been bothering you."

Izzy leaned back a little and said, "I actually didn't mind that you said that. I figured you were only saying it because you were shitfaced but I thought it was kind of sweet."

My face grew hot. "Wait, then why have you been distant then?"

Izzy sighed and said, "West, the thing that upset me was – I mean, it was the drinking."

"But I'm always drinking," I replied confusedly.

"That's kind of my point," Izzy went on. "You got so blackout wasted that I left for work, had an *entire shift*, came back and you were still drunk and passed out. I thought you had *died*. I kept thinking 'what if he vomited in his sleep and choked to death on it?' 'What if he gave himself alcohol poisoning?' I kept thinking I would come back to find you dead. You're my best friend, West... But I can't be with someone like that."

I sat there like a bombshell had just gone off. It hadn't even crossed my mind that the drinking could have been a factor in how Izzy saw me. "Wow," I replied. "I mean, I guess that's fair."

Izzy put her hand on mine and said, "I'm sorry, West. But that's just how it is."

As she finished her words, I glanced over at Clyde. Kimmy must have been saying something he didn't like because he looked heated. In a moment, he came over to us. "Hop up, Izzy," he said politely enough, but he was clearly biting back some kind of anger.

"What?" she asked.

"Give us a moment, okay?" Clyde told her. There was a deadly seriousness in his eyes. Izzy listened. Clyde didn't take a seat, but he looked at me and said, "Are you fucking my sister?"

"What?" I replied.

"It's a simple question. Are you fucking my sister?"

I shot a glance at Kimmy, who was staring at me and Clyde. That fucking cunt, she told him. I looked Clyde in his eyes, thought about lying, but I knew it was futile. "Yeah."

Clyde turned his head for a moment as his expression morphed into fury, then looked back at me and said, "Look, I'm sorry you're being blamed for shit you didn't do, alright? It sucks, and I hope you clear your name soon." He pointed forcefully at me. "But you're a deceitful piece of shit and if I see you outside of this place, I'll knock your fucking teeth down your throat. Don't talk to me. We're done."

As Clyde furiously walked out the back door of the Hole, I was left alone. In the span of a few minutes, I had alienated both of my best friends. And it was my own fucking fault.

Finally, Jordan walked into the bar. He had a limp going thanks to Clyde's handy work and a bruise across his cheek thanks to mine. He came up to me. "You ready?"

I stared at my drink and thought about what Izzy had said. I could have chosen not to finish it. I could have left it on the bar and kept a clear head. But I didn't. I downed it, let it take the pain away, then said, "Let's go."

***

Jordan led me as I followed. We walked through Matchstick in the dark, the only light coming from the dim glow of ancient street lamps and a sliver of moonlight. We walked away from the small shopping district and over toward a group of townhouses.

"This had better be leading to something," I said to Jordan.

"Fucking chill, dude," he replied. "We'll be there in a minute." I looked at him with suspicion, but he was my only option. We made our way through the rows of townhomes until we got to the very back corner.

"If you're gonna try to convince me that Fletch is just hiding out in someone's house," I began, "I'm gonna break that other fucking knee."

"He's not." Jordan stopped walking and pointed to the house furthest back. It had a sign in the yard that said condemned and caution tape across the door. "See that one back there?"

"Yeah?"

"That's where he is."

"In a condemned townhouse...?" I asked curiously.

Jordan pointed at his skull and said, "Use your fucking brain, fool. These houses have only been here for like four years, how in the hell could one of them be condemned already?"

I thought about what he was saying. "Shit, that's brilliant."

Jordan looked around sketchily and said, "Yeah, well, this is where we part ways. Don't tell Fletch I brought you here, okay?"

I nodded. "Okay." As Jordan began to limp away, I said, "Hey, sorry about your leg. And for what it's worth, I never slept with your ex." He just looked back at me for a moment, then resumed walking.

My next move was to hatch a plan. I couldn't just walk up to the door and start banging. I didn't know if Fletch was strapped, but I wasn't looking to find out. There was a car in the driveway, though. It wasn't one I had ever seen Fletch drive, but it was a known fact that he had a couple of "incognito" cars – cars that weren't technically his or that he didn't usually drive, but would use when he made drop offs and pickups. He wasn't a genius, but he wasn't a fool, either.

The car was my only angle. Quietly, under the cover of darkness, I crept up to the car, picked up a decently heavy stone, and smashed it through the passenger window. The car alarm blared beautifully – no one could ignore that. Kneeling down behind the car, I waited.

After a minute, the front door creaked open slowly. Fletch popped his head out and looked around. Seeing nobody, he deemed it safe to step out and take a look at his car. My heart pounded as Fletch went over to the driver side, unlocked the door, and leaned into the car. I saw my chance and I took it.

Rounding to the other side of the driver's door, I stood there for a second as the alarm turned off and Fletch began to withdraw from the car. But as soon as his shoulders had cleared the door, I slammed it shut on his head.

"Fuck!" Fletch cried out in pain. Quickly, I grabbed him by the shoulders, pulled him back, kicked the door shut then drove his head into the window. He hit it hard enough to crack the glass. With Fletch dazed and stunned, I threw him to the ground and pinned him down with my knee on his chest.

"Tell me what happened to Kayla!" I roared with a fist cocked back.

"I don't know anything, man!"

My fist launched into his temple. "I don't fucking believe you, Fletch. You know *something*."

"You're a fucking psycho, West!" Fletch yelled out as he struggled to get free. I hit him again.

"I'll show you how much of a fucking psycho I am!" Hit him one more time. "Why did you get in Kayla's car that night?"

"I already told you, man!"

"What the fuck would she want to go to North Carolina for?" I asked through gritted teeth. I cocked my fist back once more, ready to crack the son of a bitch's jaw. "Tell me!" The devil himself might have had a hold on me.

"To get away from you!" Fletch yelled out.

What? For some reason, I knew that Fletch believed what he was saying was true. But I couldn't understand why she would have wanted that. "Why the hell would Kayla want to get away from *me*?" I asked, letting him up.

Fletch brushed himself off and wiped the blood from his nose then stood up. "I have no idea, man, honest to god."

"Did she tell you that?"

"Kind of sort of," Fletch said in vague, slurred speech. "She didn't come outright and say it, but the implication was there."

"Then how do you know?"

Fletch seemed to really think about it before he said anything – not in a way like he was making it up on the spot, but more like deciding to break trust and burn bridges. "You should ask Kimmy."

"What?" I said with confusion. "What's she got to do with this?"

"Kimmy's tight with one of Kayla's friends – I think her name is Robin. I think. I don't know what she knows, but I know *that* she knows. Kimmy and Matilda are the ones that started the rumors. That's all I can tell you, man."

"Why would Kimmy and Matilda go around telling people I was a rapist?" I asked. "And what about the phone call?"

"I don't fuckin' know, man," Fletch replied exasperatedly. "I know Dane said he thought you were a creep. Other than that, that's it. You've reached the depths of my knowledge on this topic."

I tossed his words around in my brain for a moment. Could Kimmy really have been behind the date-rape rumors? "How do I know I can trust you? Way I see it, you're looking an awful lot like the killer to me."

Fletch let out a sigh and said, "I have an alibi."

I looked at him curiously. "Then...why are you hiding?"

At that moment, a car turned the corner. As soon as it saw us, it sped up. Fletch must have recognized the car, because he audibly said, "Fuck." It came to a screeching halt as it approached us. The headlights were blinding, but I could see the silhouette of a stocky man step out of the car.

"I fucking warned you, Fletch," he said. It was Vince.

"Bro – " Fletch began, but Vince cut him off.

"Shut up, shut the fuck up, Fletch!" Vince barreled toward us.

I held out my hand to stop him as he got closer to Fletch. "Vince? What's this about?"

"Back the fuck up, West," Vince warned me. "We're not in your bar anymore."

"Vince," Fletch started, "I promise you, whatever you think happened, didn't happen."

"Oh yeah?" Vince challenged. "So that night I came to the bar and told you to stop fucking around with my little sister, you didn't take her back to your house?" The night Vince was referring to was the same night Kayla died.

"Nah, man, I don't know what you're talking about."

I looked at Fletch. "Wait, is *that* your fucking alibi? Jesus fucking Christ, Fletch."

Fletch looked between the two of us. Neither outcome was going to be good for him. Finally, he sighed and said, "Alright, alright. I was with Maisy that night. She called me all upset and shit about you being mad, so I was there to comfort her."

The look in Vince's eyes, the twisted grin of fury and disbelief on his face – I had never seen anything like it. He scoffed and said, "Remember what I told you? Remember what I said would happen if you ever touched her again?"

Fletch timidly shook his head and started to speak. "I – " was all he had the time to say. In a flash, Vince lunged at the man and tackled him to the ground, his fists rearing back in turns and slamming down onto Fletch's face with wet cracking sounds as Fletch's head smacked the pavement.

"Vince, no!" I shouted and jumped on him, but Vince threw me back like it was nothing. He continued to beat the man's face into a pulp.

"Don't – you – ever – fucking – touch – my – sister – you piece – of fucking – *shit!*" Each word was punctuated by another blow. By the end of the sentence, Fletch had stopped moving. Huffing and panting, out of breath, Vince rose to his feet. Fletch's face was unrecognizable. His body was limp and inert. He wasn't even breathing.

Shocked, I ran my fingers through my hair and paced back and forth. "Jesus fuck, Vince. What did you do?"

Vince looked down at Fletch's body. "I gave him what he fucking deserved." As the sound of sirens began to blare in the distance, Vince jumped back into his car and drove off.

Panicked, I took one last look at Fletch's mangled face. Nobody would believe that I wasn't the one responsible if I was there when the cops showed up. So I did the only thing I could do.

I ran. I ran as fast as I could all the way back to my apartment.

My heart was still racing long after I was inside.

Without losing another moment, I grabbed a bottle of jack and drank it straight from the bottle.

Chapter 13

Kayla's funeral service was the next day. I wasn't invited.

News about Fletch's murder spread through Matchstick like wildfire. People wondered if his murder was connected to Kayla's or if our sleepy little town was quickly becoming more dangerous. There were only two people alive who knew why Fletch was killed: me and Vince. And I wasn't about to rat Vince out for killing the man who violated his teen sister.

The consequence of that, though, was people would inevitably begin to think that I did it.

Kimmy was unreachable. She wouldn't take calls and she was nowhere to be found. The poor grieving would-be widow of an abusive man who never loved her, what a fucking sight to behold. If people knew what we truly thought about each other, I suspect a lot of bars would go out of business.

It was three in the afternoon when I arrived at the Hole for work that day – three hours late for my shift. My blood was more booze than blood cells by that point and my breath reeked of whiskey.

"Where the fuck have you been?" my father asked. He wore his black suit for the funeral. "It's three in the fucking afternoon, West! You were supposed to be here at twelve! I need you to cover the bar for me while I'm at the funeral."

"Shit happens," I muttered as I drunkenly staggered into the bar.

"What the hell did you just say?" my father challenged.

"I said *shit...happens*."

"Are you *drunk*?"

"Sure seems that way, don't it, detective?" I sneered callously.

He just looked at me in disbelief. "You're a fucking mess, West. I can't let this slide anymore." He paused as he thought about his next words; they were simple: "Go home."

"Woooo," I mockingly cheered as I spun my finger in a circle in the air. "I get another day off."

"I don't think you understand me, Weston. You're fired."

"*What?*" I asked sharply.

"I said you're fired." Stoically, my father held his ground.

Disbelief painted my face as I looked at him and scoffed. "Are you fucking serious? You don't think that maybe, just *maybe*, I'm entitled to have the occasional bad fucking day?"

"That's the thing with you, West – they're *all* bad fucking days. Long before Kayla died, long before people started dragging your name through the mud. I can't let you sit here and destroy yourself anymore, okay? Get help."

My face twisted with humor and malice. "Get help?" I mocked. "For what, the – " I hiccuped, " – the fucking *drinking*? We work at a fucking *bar*, dude. Get over yourself."

"Yeah, we work at a fucking bar, yet nobody else fucking drinks on the job. You think I don't notice that shit? I'm not an idiot, West. I *raised* you. You're not even just drinking on the job – you're showing up absolutely fucking *plastered*. And I will not continue to let it slide. Get the fuck out of my bar."

The reality that he was serious began to set in. I wanted to argue back, to fight with him, but the point was moot. There wasn't anything I could do except leave. So that's what I did. "Fuck this place," I muttered as I walked out.

I paced around my apartment drinking heavily. Everyone was at Kayla's funeral. Robin, Izzy, Clyde, my father – everybody who either gave a damn about me or who might have been able to shed some light on Kayla's death, they were all just out of reach.

It was my right to be at that funeral. Nobody loved Kayla the way that I did. Even when we fought, hurt each other, cheated on each other, even through all of that, I never stopped loving her. And now she was being put in the fucking ground in a closed casket funeral. Everybody would shed their weepy tears and curse my name under their breath, while I was forced to sit there alone, ostracized from my family and community.

Fuck that.

I finished the bottle of jack and stepped into the waning daylight giving way to twilight. My car refused to steer straight while I drove, hammered off my ass. When I got to the Church of Grace, the parking lot was practically filled with people who showed up to pay their respects. And none of them even knew her like I did.

By the time I arrived, the funeral had made its way into the cemetery behind the church. I stood off at a distance at first, drinking from my flask and watching the procession. Everybody was there. Bill Sparks stood a few feet away from Izzy, Clyde, Jane, and my father. I could tell he wanted to lay into all of them and grill them about me. There was sadness in his eyes but it was overshadowed by hatred and rage. Just about everyone had tears in their eyes as the preacher delivered his sermon, everyone except for Clyde and my father. Clyde had an expression of stoic sorrow, like he was pushing down any negative feelings, but the look my father held was moving. He stared at that casket as if he had lost something incredibly special – grandchildren, his son's future, the only woman he had ever seen his boy head over heels for. He grieved as though he had truly lost something he could never get back, like he was grieving *for* me in my absence.

I couldn't watch it anymore.

The pastor said, "A life taken from us too soon, she will be missed. For whatever reasons God deemed it to take her so young, she will not be forgotten."

"Fuck that," I said from the back. Quickly, every head in the funeral turned toward me. I took another drink from my flask then tucked it back in my pocket. "God deemed it necessary?" I asked rhetorically and scoffed. "God had nothing to fucking do with this."

Rudely and unconcerned with how I came off, I pushed my way through the crowd. My dad placed his hand on my shoulder to stop me as I approached the casket. "West," he said in a low, pained voice. "Whatever the fuck you think you're about to do, don't do it."

I shirked his hand off me and said, "Get the fuck off of me," then walked up to where the pastor was standing and faced the crowd. Clyde, Izzy and Jane gave me concerned looks and tried to silently coax me away from the casket, while Bill simply glared at me with fury. "Fuck *all* of this," I blurted out. "Ninety-five percent of you fucking people didn't care about her. You had *no fucking clue* what she was going through! You weren't fucking there for her when she was alive; don't you *dare* pretend to be there for her in death. You fucking sycophants. You fucking liars. I guarantee you almost everybody here thinks I fucking did it. Thinks I killed the fucking woman that I *loved*. Well fuck that and fuck you, too. You think you people have lost something? A friend? An acquaintance? You wanna know what I fucking lost?"

My father spoke up in a voice just loud enough to be heard by me. "West, that's *enough*."

I ignored him and went on. I pointed my finger harshly at the casket. "You fucking people didn't know the real Kayla. All you saw was the bubbly and quirky woman on the surface. None of you *ever* saw the ugly side. Well I fucking *did*, and I fucking loved her for it anyway." I took a breath as tears began to sting my eyes. "Nobody else fucking knew her like me. Nobody else loved her like me. The good, the bad – all of it."

Bill erupted. "God damn it, West, get the fuck away from my daughter!"

"Fuck you, Bill! Where were you, huh? Your own fucking daughter was afraid for her life. She was so afraid she was ready to move a thousand miles away. Did you know that? Did any of you fucking know that?! Where were you, Bill? Why didn't you protect her?" I glared at him as he returned daggers with his eyes. "Where were you?" I began to choke. Quietly, I said, "Where was I?" I stifled tears and choked again before finally saying, "Rest in peace, Kayla. And the rest of us? We can all burn in hell."

With that, I began to move back toward the crowd. Clyde stopped me. "What the fuck was that, West?"

"Fuck you, Clyde."

As the words left my mouth, a memory hit me. The first time I went to a bar after my twenty-first birthday, the bartender didn't believe my ID was legit, so he told me I could have anything non-alcoholic. So I took my ID back and said fuck you. When I told my dad that story later that night, he told me to step outside. As soon as we were out there, he rushed me and tackled me to the ground. I squirmed out of his grip and got a couple of blows on him, but without a lot of effort he overpowered me and knocked me to the ground. I had a bruised rib for probably a month and a half after that. As I laid on the ground, my father told me, "See that? *That's* what it means when you say 'fuck you' to somebody. If you're not ready to throw down or get your ass beat, then don't ever say it."

Turns out it was good advice.

"Fuck me?" Clyde said as anger rose in his throat. Immediately, his suit coat was on the grass. "No, fuck *you*, West." He grabbed me by my shirt and threw my ass into the dirt, then hit me in the face a couple times. I kicked him off and tried to lunge at him, but I was so fucking wasted I could barely control my body. He moved past me and sent me tumbling before cracking me in the face again. After a second, my father jumped in and pulled Clyde off of me.

"Knock it the fuck off!" he commanded. I pushed myself back up to my feet as my father held out a hand to pull me up. I knocked his hand away.

"Fuck this funeral, fuck this town, and fuck you people," I said as I stumbled off.

I was furiously intoxicated by that point and my thoughts had ceased to make sense. But I knew that I wanted blood. As I stumbled back to my apartment and tumbled through the doorway, my feet dragged me to the toilet so I could bend over and retch and gag as the contents of my stomach spewed out. I vomited until it hurt and nothing could come up anymore. Then I dry heaved some more.

Whiskey washed the taste of puke out of my mouth despite my stomach's screaming protest. I didn't care if it killed me, I wanted to blackout. To not be there. As I staggered through my apartment, I saw the roses I had bought for Izzy. All they were now was a painful reminder of my friendships dying faster than the flowers even could. I didn't know if I was in love with her, but it sure fucking felt like it. And she would never see the roses.

In a gust of loathing, I snatched the bouquet up off the table and carried it outside, grabbed a gascan from my neighbor's open shed – I didn't give a shit if they saw me or not – then tossed the roses on the gravel parking lot behind my apartment building and doused them in gas. As they soaked the bitter smelling gasoline into the flower petals, I pulled a small book of matches from my pocket, struck one, and tossed it on the roses.

They went up in flames. The smoke was thin and black and the petals took a few moments to wilt and blacken from the flame. I stared down at those burning roses and felt all of the hope die within me.

If Matchstick wanted me to be the villain, then I'd show them a real fucking villain.

***

For hours that night, I drove around drinking a six pack of Perpetual, drinking it almost as fast as I was driving. All of my windows were down, my seatbelt was off, the music was blaring and I was driving faster than the devil could run. I was more intoxicated than I think I had ever been in my entire life.

My feelings oscillated between rage and apathy. One moment I wouldn't give a damn about anything in the world, the next I would just want to watch the world burn to ashes. For reasons I couldn't fathom, I took out my phone and began to send Izzy videos on Snapchat, just blurry and sloppy recordings of myself drinking and headbanging to music while I drove around the backwoods of Coal County. I didn't know why; maybe it was because I felt spurned by her. Maybe I just missed her. Either way, I wanted to drown out the pain. I began to shout the words, "Ozzy never dies!" but the video ended abruptly.

As I flew down Winding Hill road, one of the sharp turns caught me by surprise and my car careened toward someone's yard at seventy miles an hour. My reflexes were too slow to stop what was about to happen but still fast enough to see what I was going to hit. Dead in front of me, maybe thirty or forty feet away, was an oak tree in somebody's yard, and I was about to blast through their yard in an instant. My life was over. I couldn't survive that collision.

But in an ironic twist of fate, something slowed me down just enough to give my brakes time to work.

In the center of the yard I plowed through was a wooden crucifix, buried deeply enough into the ground to slow my car a bit but made of weak enough wood for my car to break through. That extra half second that hitting the cross bought me was just enough time for my car to come to a dead stop mere inches in front of the tree.

Shaken, I backed out of the yard and sped off, driving in silence, wondering how close I had just come to losing my life.

But soon enough, all the feelings of anger, rage and regret came creeping back in. I should have just gone home, but I didn't. Instead, I went to the Hole. Sitting in my car in the parking lot, the murderous fury raged inside of me. I thought back to the time when I was a young child, sitting in the car with my father. He was mad about something – who the fuck ever knew with him – and for a while, he just sat there, brewing. Then, almost out of nowhere, he erupted into a furious scream and launched his fist into the dashboard of his car over and over until every piece of it was cracked and broken. I thought back to that time as I let out my own cry of rage and shot my fist into my dash until pieces of plastic fell to the floor and my knuckles bled.

But it wasn't enough. I needed to get out of the car. I needed something more.

The bar had been closed all night since I wasn't there to man it while everyone else was at the funeral. I thought about how they all had the luxury of not being the villain in the story. They got to mourn the loss that no one should have mourned more than me, with the possible exception of Kayla's father. Clyde had beaten me into the ground like it was nothing. My father had taken my livelihood from me. Kayla's father wanted to pin me for murder.

They could all get fucked.

Rage boiled inside of me as I unlocked the door to the tavern. Clyde wouldn't forgive me for lying to him, for fucking his sister. And he would take every chance he could to knock my ass in the dirt. I was already looking over my shoulder constantly – I couldn't fucking take having another enemy.

So in my drunken state I decided to take action.

Surprisingly dextrous for my level of inebriation, I hopped over the bar and pulled the handgun from its position of safe keeping. It was a loaded .38 special revolver, with a heavy weight in my hand. It was like an immediate rush, like knowing that suddenly I had power in place of weakness. With that fucking gun, I could do whatever I wanted.

I didn't have to be afraid anymore.

Drunkenly, bordering blackout territory yet somehow still conscious, I aimed the pistol around the bar. I pictured the people I would unload it on. Whoever killed Kayla. Whoever made that phone call pretending to be a police officer. Whoever started the rumors. And, in that moment, whoever thought they could lay a hand on me – Clyde.

As the humiliation of my public beating replayed in my mind, I squeezed the trigger of the revolver. A loud crack boomed through the bar as the bullet embedded itself in the brick wall. I liked the way it felt. So I fired it again. And again. And again. Recklessly, carelessly, unconcerned with the damage or the consequences as I quickly snapped toward the entrance to fire one more round.

But then I saw something that stopped my heart and stole my breath. As my finger went to squeeze the trigger one more time, I realized that there was a person standing in the doorway, directly in front of me. Directly in front of the revolver.

It was Izzy.

She screamed as the gunshot rang out in the bar.

Chapter 14

"No!" I screamed as I realized what I had done. Izzy clasped her hands over her ears and fell to her knees and in an instant I jumped over the bar and ran to her. Please god tell me I missed. Those few moments where I was just cognizant enough to know what I had done were the worst moments of my life. Everything ended in a split second. If I hurt Izzy – if I killed her – I couldn't have lived with myself. "Please, please tell me you're okay," I said frantically as I knelt down beside her.

Frightened and shaken, Isabella slowly pulled her hands away from her ears as she sat on the ground quivering. I couldn't see any sort of wounds on her, but in one of the support beams right to the side of and behind her was a bullet hole, splintering the wood. At long last, she finally said, "I'm... I'm okay, West."

I breathed a guilt-ridden sigh of relief. "Thank god. What are you doing here?"

"After I saw those snaps you sent me and everything that happened at the funeral, I thought I'd check on you. You weren't at your apartment, so I figured this was the most likely place you'd be."

"I'm so sorry," I slurred in speech full of remorse. My arms went to wrap around her, but she pushed me back.

"Please," she pleaded softly, "please... don't. Just don't." With those words, she got to her feet, turned around and walked out of the bar. Sitting there on that floor alone in the Hole in the Ground, that was the most despondent, the absolute loneliest and most hopeless I had ever been. I thought about everything that had happened, everything that I had turned into. A man with no friends and no good name. Clyde's words rang in my ears. Can't let the bottle be your best friend. It'll get you into all sorts of trouble.

For the first time in my life, I understood something: I had a problem.

But it was deeper than that. I didn't just *have* a problem, I *was* the problem. I had drank and fucked my way through misery and all it did was bring more misery to my door.

And I was fucking sick of it.

I walked out of the bar with the gun still in my hand, got into my car, stashed the pistol in the glove compartment, and drove. At first I wasn't sure where I was going, but after just a minute my destination became clear. And for the first time, I was the one steering the wheel.

It was nearly a thirty minute drive with no traffic to the city of Antioch, the closest thing to a real city in Coal County. But soon enough, I saw my destination.

In glowing, bright letters on an electric billboard, a sign read: MEMORIAL HOSPITAL.

As I sat in my car nervously puffing on a cigarette, I sent a text to Izzy: "I'm so fucked up right now I don't even know how to form a sentence. But I think I've lost my mind. I'm gonna be out of reach for the next few days. I'm really sorry for everything I've put you through. Maybe someday we can try again. I really, really liked you."

With that, I tossed the cigarette, turned off my phone and stored it in the center console. I wouldn't need it where I was going.

The sliding glass doors opened as I stepped into the emergency room. A kindly looking woman sat behind a desk and asked, "Hi, can I help you?"

"My name is Weston Ryder. I need to check myself into crisis prevention."

"Can you tell me a little about what's going on?" she said as she began to enter information into her computer. I was sore. I was tired. I was defeated.

"I've become a danger to myself. And others."

PART TWO:
SOBERING THOUGHTS

Chapter 15

Nobody likes hospitals. Not even the people who work there.

I sat in an uncomfortably stiff chair as a nurse took my vitals and asked me questions.

"You wanna tell me a little bit about what's going on?" she asked in a soothing voice.

"Long story short I just went on a shooting spree and I'm pretty sure I'm losing it."

"A shooting spree?" she asked in a voice like a teacher would ask a child about a drawing. "What happened?"

"Nobody was hurt," I told her immediately. "But I got drunk and stole my dad's gun and began firing it in random directions." Guilt twinged through me. "I almost hit a friend of mine."

"Why did you start shooting, West?"

"I thought I might have to kill a friend." Sorry, Clyde.

"How often do you drink?"

"Daily."

"How much do you usually drink in a day?"

"Probably about five or six mixed drinks, usually either jack or captain, maybe half a dozen beers, a few shots."

"You mean it's usually either a few mixed drinks or a few beers or – ?"

"No, I mean it's usually all of the above."

"Wow, well that certainly is a lot. Are you still feeling intoxicated?"

"I'm definitely still a little drunk," I admitted, "but I think I'm sobering up."

"Okay, well that's good at least. Have you ever used drugs not prescribed to you by a doctor?"

"Almost exclusively."

The nurse laughed then finished checking my vitals and said, "Everything looks normal, physiologically speaking, so that's good. We should have a bed open in the Behavioral Health Unit in a few hours. Until then, we're going to have you sit in a room with one of our triage nurses so they can monitor you, okay?"

"Don't worry, I'm not going anywhere."

"That's what they all say," the nurse chuckled. A security guard walked through the door. The nurse asked him, "Can you come with us so we can get Weston here changed into hospital clothes?"

"Sure," the guard said.

The nurse rose to her feet and said, "Alright, Weston, if you can just follow us." The pair led me through the labyrinthian corridors of the hospital wing, full of nurses and doctors and orderlies hurrying about, chatting about their minimal social lives and trying to stay positive through long and arduous shifts until we arrived at a small room with hospital gowns sealed in individual plastic bags. "Okay," the nurse said, "if you wanna go ahead and step in here and change for me, we'll get your clothes washed and sent up to the B-Unit. I can turn around to give you some privacy but, unfortunately – for safety reasons – we can't let you close this door."

"Believe me," I began, "enough people have seen me naked for it to not bother me anymore." The nurse laughed again then turned around while I disrobed. The hospital gown was somehow both breezy *and* uncomfortable, like wearing the curtain a barber puts over you with nothing on underneath. The trousers were baggy and starchy, uncomfortably rubbing against my dick every time I moved. But the worst part was the socks. They were these strangely shaped grippy things that were designed to fit at any orientation, meaning they didn't quite fit right any way you put them on. They were thin, dark green, and ungodly uncomfortable. The entire outfit ran the gamut of shades of green, and as soon as I saw myself in the mirror I realized I looked like a fucking crazy person. "No points for style, I guess."

"Alright," the nurse said as she turned back around, "We're gonna go ahead and take you to the room you'll be staying in tonight until they get your bed ready upstairs, okay?"

She took me to a fairly small room with a hospital bed, some equipment, and a TV mounted on the wall that got a whopping three channels. After a couple minutes, another nurse strolled in and said, "Okay I'm here, you're good to go." The first nurse left and I sat there in mostly silence with the new one as some crime dramas played out on TV. They called the nurse watching me the "sitter," like the babysitter. As if the constant soothing voices and borderline child-speak wasn't patronizing enough.

I didn't want to be there. My mind went back to Kayla, back to the reality that she was dead and I still didn't know why. I wanted to leave, to get back out there and keep searching for answers. But I wasn't ever going to find the truth in the state I was in.

You don't know how fucking slowly time ticks by until you've sat in a hospital bed doing nothing for twelve hours. They brought me some sort of powdered egg with cheap bacon for dinner and trying to understand what the fuck that meal was was the most excitement I had the entire time I was in that room. I was sober again, and my only urge was to get a drink. I wanted *something*. I wanted to be high, I wanted to be drunk, I wanted one of the prettier nurses to walk in and suck me off like I was living in a porno. I wanted anything that would distract me from the fact that I had self-destructed my way all the way to a hospital room. But no reprieve would come. There was only one way out of that hospital – progress. Eventually, my restlessness subsided just enough to sleep for a couple of hours until I finally awoke to another security man and a new nurse standing over me.

"Weston?" the nurse said as I awoke. "Your bed in the B-Unit is ready now, we're gonna go ahead and take you upstairs, okay?"

"Already?" I remarked sarcastically. "And here I was finally starting to enjoy my life in this room." The security guard led the way as the nurse wheeled my bed through the maze of hallways through doors and elevators. Thank christ I wasn't left to my own devices because I wouldn't have found my way out of that hospital in a million fucking years. After a few minutes, we arrived at a hallway that had the words B-UNIT printed above a heavy metal double door that only opened with security clearance. For the first time since I had arrived, I felt fear – fear of what awaited me on the other side, fear of what the doctors might want to do. Fear of never being able to leave.

But I had brought myself there for a reason, and I intended to see it through – I was completely cut off from drugs and alcohol. I needed to detox. I needed help.

Once we were through those doors, I wasn't going to be able to leave until the doctors let me. And as those heavy metal doors closed behind me, I wondered if I had made the right decision.

***

The first day in B-Unit was the worst. About half of the twenty-five or so in-patients wore those uncomfortable green hospital clothes, and the other half wore their pajamas. The B-Unit was reserved for mental health problems regarding depression, suicide, drug addiction, and bipolar disorder. Apparently, A-Unit was where the real shit happened – I called it the Thorazine unit, because that's where the psychotically deranged went to mentally castrated by copious amounts of pharmaceuticals. To be honest, there were times where I felt they had put me in the wrong ward.

The nurse showed me to my room. My roommate was sitting in his bed borderline catatonically, hugging himself and gently rocking back and forth with a goofy grin on his face. He was a big man with dark skin, either mixed race or native american, I couldn't tell which. I never learned his name, so I just called him Chief, like the character in *One Flew Over the Cuckoo's Nest*. The room was just big enough to not be uncomfortable, and it's what I would call "suicide proof." There was no ledge or anything to hang yourself from, nothing remotely sharp or dangerous, cages on the windows and a paper curtain over the bathroom. Even the pencils were soft and bendy, which also made them actually fucking useless to write with. I got a little basket with baby shampoo and body wash, some deodorant, and a non-lethal toothbrush – something I didn't think was lethal in the first place.

B-Unit was like a playground for the mentally disturbed. It was essentially a hallway with several rooms on either side. There was the office, protected by plexiglas and locked doors; the recreation room that basically housed puzzles and coloring books and doubled as the cafeteria for when they would bring in the food three times a day; there was the meeting room, filled with the only comfortable furniture in the entire goddamn unit; and there were the bedrooms, each one being large enough to accommodate two to three people. One girl walked back and forth endlessly through the hallway, counting laps to herself as she stiffly walked. A few people sat in small groups, some just talking, some playing cards, some just sitting there. And through it all there was always a couple of nurses with their rolling computer terminals close by.

It felt like a fucking mad house. Even the windows made you feel crazy, because B-Unit was one of the oldest parts of the hospital and, since it was built, there had been numerous additions built around it – meaning every single one of the fucking windows looked out directly to the exterior of a brick wall. It was like a sick joke. If you didn't feel crazy before, you sure as shit did now.

I went over and sat with a pretty girl who looked about nineteen or twenty in the rec room. She sat with a sheet draped over her shoulders for comfort. "Hey," I said.

"Don't talk to me."

"Um... Okay." So I got up and moved to a different seat, this time around a couple of guys around my age, an older woman, and a woman who looked about thirty. "Well this is fucking weird," I said as I sat down.

"First time?" one of the guys said. He was tall with dark curly hair and also had a sheet wrapped around himself.

"Is this *not* your first time?" I asked.

The other guy laughed. He was short and stocky, wore normal clothes, had blonde hair, and spoke with a slight lisp. "Most of us come here a lot," he said.

"Well that's...fucking depressing," I replied grimly. Everybody at the table let out a laugh.

The older woman spoke. "What are you in here for?"

"Same as you, probably," I replied vaguely. "I went crazy."

"Boy," she replied, "I done went crazy a *long* time ago."

"How long do they usually keep people here?" I asked hesitantly.

The blonde guy replied. "All depends on the person. Me, for example – I've been here for almost three months."

"*Three months?!*" I blurted. "I can't stay here for three months, I've got shit to do!"

The dark haired guy chuckled and said, "Chill, man, chill. They'll probably just keep you for a couple days if you've got a home to go back to. Most of us who've been in here a while don't really have anywhere else to go. I'm Nic, by the way."

"Oh, shit," I said apologetically. "I'm sorry. I'm Weston."

The blonde guy said, "I'm Dustin, this is Claire, and this is Liz." He gestured to the older woman and the younger woman, respectively. "Welcome to B-Unit."

I looked at him and said, "I notice you're not wearing this god fucking awful hospital gown. Any chance I'm gonna get my clothes back before I die?"

Dustin chuckled and said, "Probably by tomorrow. They take their sweet time with the laundry."

"Great," I replied dismally. At that moment, a nurse strolled into the rec room.

"Alright, everybody," she started. "We're gonna go ahead and start today's activity. Anybody who wants to participate is welcome to join."

"Activity?" I asked Dustin quietly. "What, like coloring?"

"You're not too far off."

The nurse went on as the room filled up with patients. "Nic, would you like to pass out the activity sheets to everybody?"

"Yes, ma'am," Nic said as he got up and took a stack of papers from her, handing one to each person.

I asked Dustin, "Do I get a pencil or are we using magic markers?"

"Crayons," he replied. "Either that or you can use one of the bendy pencils."

"You mean the shockingly non-lethal pencils?"

"Exactly."

"Fantastic."

The nurse explained the activity as I looked at the paper, containing only a very crude drawing of the checkout conveyor at a grocery store. "Okay, so today we're going to do a money management activity. Now, I want each of you to imagine I just gave you a hundred dollars to spend at the grocery store. I want you all to write down what you would buy with that hundred dollars."

Obediently, everybody began to scribble shit down in crayon while I looked around in confusion. I looked at the nurse and said, "And...?"

"That's it," she said simply. "Just write down what you would buy. You can draw pictures if you want."

Thank god I wasn't suicidal when I went or I might have killed myself right there on the spot – shoved the crayons so far up my nose that they pierced my brain and the sweet bliss of hemorrhage would take me away.

After a few minutes, the nurse said, "Okay, is everybody finished?" The room murmured their confirmations. "Good! Who would like to share what they wrote?"

Nic went first. "I would give the hundred dollars to my nephew and his family," he said. "So that they could buy whatever they needed."

"Wow, good answer, Nic!" the nurse said, despite Nic's egregious misunderstanding of the assignment. It was like I was in an episode of The Twilight Zone. I could hear Rod Serling talk in my head: *Take, if you will, a man; A man who, after suffering a mental breakdown, finds himself trapped within another world – not another world of dimension, but another world of insanity; A world in which grown adults attend a kindergarten class for the mentally disturbed; A world where the sanest man in the room is the only one who is truly insane; A world we call...The Twilight Zone.*

Claire answered next. "I'm really good at money management," she started. "I would get paper towels, three boxes of off brand mac and cheese, half a gallon of milk, sirloin cut steaks – a four pack – and a half pound of broccoli, a..." she prattled on and on for three minutes straight, remarkably unaware of the fact that she surpassed a hundred dollars a quarter of the way through her list.

"Very good, Claire!" the nurse said cheerfully, ignoring the fact that the woman had listed at least three hundred dollars worth of shit. "Weston, would you like to share?"

I grunted and said, "I'd buy a hundred dollars worth of food. I mean, it's a grocery store."

"Oh?" she replied, slightly caught off guard. "What kind of food?"

"The kind you can eat."

"Okay, well that's a pretty fair response." After a few more minutes, she told us we could keep our papers or throw them away, then left the room.

"What the fuck was the point of that?" I asked Dustin.

"No idea," he shrugged. "But it passes the time."

That's all that unit was – passing the time. We played cards for a couple of hours until the food cart arrived. Since

I hadn't gotten there early enough to specify an order, I got a standard cheeseburger. It was the saddest thing I'd ever fucking seen. It made McDonald's look like a three star restaurant. But a man will eat anything if he's hungry enough so I scarfed it down.

It was lights out at nine in the evening, far fucking earlier than I was accustomed to sleeping. I didn't even get to talk to a doctor that first day. So I took my ass to bed and laid there while I tried to fall asleep. Chief snored something fucking fierce, like a mixture between sleep apnea and literal fucking screaming. "God fucking dammit," I muttered as his bizarre sounds kept me from falling asleep. I hadn't slept without being drunk in years, and I didn't know if I could actually do it anymore. But I didn't have a choice. In a frustrated huff, I grabbed my medical grade pillow and one-thread-count sheet and walked into the hallway, put my pillow on the cold floor, and laid there.

Eventually, the night duty nurse walked by. "You okay, Weston?"

"My guy in there snores," I replied. "I'm just gonna sleep out here."

She gave me a confused look, then just shrugged and said, "Alright, let me know if you need anything."

After several hours, I was asleep.

And as I thought about everything going on in Matchstick, I wondered again if I had made a mistake.

Chapter 16

"So tell me about what brought you here?" Dr. Sylvester asked as he sat across from me in a small room.

"Long story short, I've noticed an increasingly destructive pattern of reckless and impulsive behavior. Driving through people's yards, fighting, shooting guns in public spaces. That kind of thing."

"Is this a new occurrence for you or has this type of thing happened before?"

I thought about it for a second and then said, "This definitely isn't my first rodeo."

"What about depression?" he asked as he took notes.

"I've definitely experienced it before. Not right now, though. If anything, I'm kinda fucking irritable right now. I just want to stay away from alcohol for a few days so I can go back and fix some of the things I've fucked up." I thought about Kayla. I thought about Izzy. I thought about Clyde. I thought about my father. I had a lot of amends to make. I wanted out of there as soon as possible. I wanted to know what happened to Kayla. I wanted to know that I didn't do it.

"Well, by the sound of it, I believe a Bipolar type one diagnosis fits. I'm going to start you out on lithium and titrate you up or down to a dosage that works for you. We'll need to keep you here for a couple of weeks to check the levels in your blood to make sure the dosage is safe."

"No," I replied flatly.

"No?"

"First off," I began, "I'm not bipolar. I'm a raging fuckin' alcoholic. And second, I'm not staying here for another two weeks. I'm leaving tomorrow. Give me something if you have to, but make it something that I can take that won't require supervision."

He looked at me a little puzzled, but then acquiesced. "Well, I stand by my diagnosis but if you want to see how your behavior changes with sobriety, I support that. In that case, we can start you on quetiapine – also known as Seroquel. It's an atypical antipsychotic that also acts as a sedative. Does that sound agreeable to you?"

"Sure thing, Doc." I had been sober for well over twenty-four hours by that point, a new record for me. My body felt like shit, my mind felt like shit, and my life looked like shit. I just wanted to get out of there.

As I left the small room, a nurse approached me and said, "Weston, your clothes are finished. We put them in your room for you whenever you want to change."

"Thank the fucking maker," I replied and hurried into my room. Chief was nowhere to be found, so I took my clothes out of the plastic bags the staff put them in and quickly threw them on. Finally, I felt some semblance of normalcy returning.

As I walked out of my room and over to the rec room, Dustin looked at me and said, "Oh my *god*."

"What?" I asked.

"You were good looking before," he began, "but now you are drop dead *gorgeous*."

I laughed genuinely for the first time since I went there and said, "Well thanks." I didn't know if he was hitting on me or not – I actually hadn't realized he was gay until that point – but either way it felt nice to look like myself again. Nic roamed through the halls with Liz. "What's up with them?" I asked. "They spend an awful lot of time together."

Dustin looked over at them and said, "Oh, yeah, they're trying to date. Liz is actually my cousin and I've been trying to hook them up ever since she got here."

"Huh," I breathed. "Do people hook up a lot in here...?"

Dustin shot me a look and said, "Like you wouldn't fucking believe."

In the day and a half that I had been there, several of the faces had changed. People left, people came in. It was a revolving door of strange faces and broken spirits. That night a bunch of us sat in the room with the comfortable furniture as movies played on the TV.

"I don't care how old I am," Claire said, "Tom Cruise can get it any fuckin' day of the week."

Dustin laughed uproariously and said, "Me first, bitch!"

Everybody laughed at that. "Tom Cruise ain't shit," Nic said. "I've seen some shit. Tom Cruise can't imagine the shit I've been through."

"Like what?" I asked.

"Prison," Nic said. "I was there for seven years."

"Holy shit, really?" I asked. I hadn't pegged him for an ex-con.

Claire answered before Nic could: "Bitch, you were a *guard*, your ass wasn't *in* prison."

Nic was the only one not laughing. He said, "You don't know what it's like. Being a guard and being an inmate aren't very different."

"Bull-*shit*," Claire rejoined. "I've been an inmate and lemme tell you, it ain't nothing like being a guard."

"You were an inmate at a women's prison, it's different," Nic replied.

Chief, who hadn't said a single word since I got there, finally spoke. "The fuck it is," he said. We all looked at him. "Man, I was in prison. Guards get to go home. We don't."

"I was working twelve hour shifts, I barely got to go home," Nic still tried to argue his stance.

Chief chuckled then said, "Man, I will throw you over the fuckin' wall if you wanna go home so bad." We all laughed again, then the nurse came in and turned off the TV and sent everybody to bed.

They gave me a Seroquel pill right before I went to bed and I took it. It only took a few minutes for it to start to knock me out, and as I fell asleep, I realized that for the first time in a decade, I had a good time while being sober. I laughed, I was friendly, I listened and I spoke. I had a good time – something I didn't know was possible to do without alcohol.

As I fell asleep, I knew for the first time in my life that I didn't have to drink anymore.

I was ready.

***

The next morning I sat down with one of the nurses as she laid out the dos and don'ts of bipolar disorder. She gave me a sheet with advice and doctors' numbers on it, wrote me a prescription to continue taking the Seroquel, and told me I could leave at four. It was bizarre, but when the moment finally came to leave, I almost didn't want to. When you're locked in a hallway for three days, the walls start to become your friends. When I got there, I thought the girl who walked back and forth continuously was crazy. By the time I left, I had done over a thousand laps down that hall. She wasn't crazy. She was passing the time.

"You're getting out today?" Nic asked me.

"That's what they tell me."

Dustin said, "Take care of yourself out there, West. Try not to come back, but if you do – you'll probably still have friends here."

I laughed and said, "I certainly hope not. But thank you, guys. You made my visit here...tolerable."

The nurse came up and said, "West, are you ready to go?"

I took one last look at my vacation destination. In a bizarre way, it was nice to get away from the shit in Matchstick. I hadn't stopped thinking about it the entire time I was there, but I had something that I lacked three days ago.

Clarity.

"I'm ready," I said. She led me through those heavy metal doors and out to the entrance of the hospital.

As the sunlight dazzled my eyes for the first time in half a week, I took a deep breath. Kimmy was my only lead, and after Fletch's murder, I didn't know how receptive she would be to answering questions. But I wasn't going to stop.

There was work to be done.

Chapter 17

My car was exactly where I had left it with my phone still in the console. When I turned it on I was greeted with a shitstorm of notifications. There were about a hundred missed calls from my father and a few text messages from people asking me where the hell I went. I didn't respond to any of them. All I wanted to do was get back to Matchstick and end this nightmare once and for all.

I could finally have a fucking cigarette as I drove back to my town. They don't let you smoke in the psych ward, as if the twisted fates that brought you there weren't already enough cruelty. But as I got back into town, I suddenly wasn't so sure where to go.

Instinctively, I went back to the Hole. I didn't know if it was because I wanted a drink or if it was to see my friends and family, but I found myself sitting outside in my car. Something stopped me from getting out and walking in, though. There would be the consequences from my father for stealing his gun and shooting up his bar, sure. But what really stopped me was the thought of seeing Izzy in there. I almost shot her. Because of me, she nearly lost her life. The bullet missed her by an inch. There was no amount of mental preparation in the world that could let me face that shame.

So I drove away. I didn't know where I was going, but I was going. Part of me wanted to go home and simply sleep, but I had lost too much time already. Kayla's body was three days in the ground and I was no closer to finding out why than I had been four days ago. As if on its own, my hands steered the car to where I needed to be.

I came to a stop in front of Bill Sparks' house. His patrol car sat in the driveway. Word was that he had been given time off after Kayla was killed. I couldn't even imagine how he was using it.

Bracing myself, I took a breath and stepped out of the car, walked up to his door and knocked. I could still turn around and leave, I thought to myself. I didn't *have* to face him.

But I needed to.

After a moment, the door opened. Bill stood there looking haggard and weary, with a grim look of permanent anger and sadness painted on his face. He looked me up and down. "I thought you died," Bill said flatly.

"We should be so lucky."

I expected him to turn me away, to berate me, to beat the everloving shit out of me. But he didn't do any of those things. Instead, he turned around and walked away, saying unenthusiastically, "Come on in."

Hesitantly, I pushed through the screen door. I hadn't been at Bill's house in probably a year. It was a nice place, though it could use a woman's touch. Kayla's parents had divorced way back when she was nine or ten. The fact that I couldn't remember which age it was made me feel all the more guilty. "I don't really know how to start this off," I said nervously as we entered the sparse living room. "Christ I could use a drink," I said more to myself than him.

"You're not already drunk?" Bill asked harshly and scoffed. "That's a first."

"Won't be a last, either," I replied. "I'm sober now."

"I got that you're sober right now when you said you weren't drunk," Bill remarked rudely.

"No, I mean I'm *sober*. I don't drink anymore."

Bill eyed me curiously. "No shit?" he asked genuinely. "How long?"

"Since the funeral." Both of our eyes fell as I mentioned Kayla's service.

"Well, congratu-fucking-lations I guess. Why are you here, West?"

"To be honest," I began, "I don't really know. I didn't know where else to go."

"You could start with your own fuckin' home." Bill sat himself down on an armchair.

I took a seat across from him on the sofa. "Bill, I'm sorry."

"For what?" he asked.

"For fucking everything. For the way I acted at the funeral. For what I said to you. For getting Kayla involved in the neverending shitshow that is my life. She deserved better than a barfly in Matchstick."

"We finally agree on something, then." Bill leaned forward. "Look, West – I don't like you. Never have. Never liked your old man either. I think you're a lowlife, good for nothing, smart mouthed little shit."

"Wow, thanks, man," I replied with bitter sarcasm.

"But I don't think you're a killer."

My eyes lit up with surprise. "What?" I asked, astonished.

"I've seen killers, West. I've met them. Talked to them. They've got this look in their eyes, like there's blackness where the soul ought to be." The old woman's words to Kayla about me popped in my head. "You've got your issues, for sure. But you ain't a killer."

"Then what do you think happened?" I asked.

"To be honest? No fucking clue. I've been walking around with a fury and a rage so bad I can't hardly fucking think straight. But I know that detective hasn't turned up shit yet."

"They don't have any leads?" I asked.

"Not as far as I know. Why? Do you know something?"

I racked my brain for all of the information I could. "I'm still trying to stitch together what happened. I thought it was Fletch at first, but before he died it was made pretty clear he had an alibi."

"Which was?"

"Banging somebody's underage sister," I told him. Bill's face twisted with disgust. "Yeah, he got what he deserved."

"What else do you know?"

"I know that Fletch's girlfriend, Kimmy, started a rumor that I had been putting roofies in girls' drinks, that I was a rapist. I know she told a few people and those people told other people, until someone called a bunch of local bars posing as a cop and said I had been arrested for rape. I actually thought it was you. There's this guy named Neil, too. He was the first person to say something about it, and I was thinking he might have made the calls. But I don't know why he would want to frame me for something like that, so I've kind of ruled him out as a suspect."

Bill scratched his chin as though something about the phone call sparked a thought or a memory, but said, "That's not something I would do. I respect the law and innocent until proven guilty. If you had actually been busted for some shit like that, I'd tell everyone in a heartbeat. But I wouldn't make it up. I'll look into the phone calls, though. See what I can find out."

"Yeah, go figure," I muttered defeatedly.

"So Kimmy's your only lead?" Bill asked.

"Unfortunately. I think if we find her, we can find the guy who called in the false rape allegations. And if we find him, we might be able to figure out what happened to Kayla."

"Why do you think they're connected?"

I let out a deep breath and said, "Because I think I'm being framed. I think this was all done deliberately to set me up as the killer. Why else would they put Kayla's body behind the Hole in the Ground?"

Bill stroked the stubble on his chin and said, "You might actually have a point there." Abruptly, he got to his feet and walked away.

I got up after him and said, "Where are you going?"

"To go find Kimmy. And you're coming with me."

***

Bill drove us through town slowly in his cruiser while I rode shotgun. It was an SUV with a large interior. The dashboard was decked out with all sorts of equipment, including a mounted reinforced laptop. I glanced to my side to see an AR-15 stashed by the door.

"Jesus," I muttered.

"What?"

"Nothing," I said, "it's just weird not being in handcuffs for a change. I don't know if you've ever had to sit on your hands for half an hour, but normally the ride in these things is pretty fucking uncomfortable."

"Well don't get used to it. I give it three weeks before you're off the wagon and back in handcuffs."

"Gee, thanks, Sparky," I remarked. Bill glared at me. "Alright," I said, "I'll stop calling you Sparky if you promise not to arrest me anymore."

"Why did I bring you along?" Bill rolled his eyes.

"Because I'm the son you never had?"

"You're the son I never wanted." We pulled into a neighborhood that I hadn't spent too much time in before.

"Where are we?" I asked.

Bill looked at me like I was an idiot and said, "Seriously? You've lived here for your entire life and you don't know where we are?"

"I mean I know the fucking street name, I meant *why* are we here."

"This is where Kimmy lives, you dumbass."

"Well excuse the fuck out of me, I don't hang out with every random stray that walks through the Hole."

The car pulled up to a house and stopped along the curb. Bill spoke. "Alright, I'm not sure how exactly we go about this."

"You mean asking Kimmy questions?"

"It's more complicated than that," Bill explained. "She has to feel both comforted and pressured at the same time. It's not as easy as it looks in movies."

"Considering her experience with Fletch, I doubt she'll be willing to talk to a cop. But maybe just knowing you're involved will be enough to pressure her into talking."

"So you want to take the lead on this one?"

"I think that's the best option we have."

Bill sighed, thought about it for a second, then told me, "Okay. Just don't fuck it up, or I swear to god – "

"Believe me," I interrupted him. "Whatever you could do to me will pale in comparison to what I would do to myself if I don't find out what happened." I took a deep breath then stepped out of the car and walked up to Kimmy's door. My fist rapped loudly but gently against the wood. After a moment, an older woman appeared.

"Can I help you?" she asked.

"I was wondering if Kimmy was here?" I said, caught off guard. I didn't realize she still lived with her parents, although it made sense. Fletch would never put her name on the lease for his own house, so with him out of the picture she would have nowhere else to go.

"No, she's not home," Kimmy's mother replied.

"Any idea where she is?"

"I'm not sure, she didn't say." The woman glanced at the police cruiser. "She isn't in any trouble, is she?"

"No," I told her. "I just wanted to pass along my condolences about Fletch."

The mother clicked her tongue and said, "If I had to take a guess, I'd say she's at the Hole in the Ground Tavern. I think she's with Dane and Matilda."

My gut tightened a bit. "Alright, thank you, ma'am. I really appreciate it." As the door closed, I walked back to the car.

"Well?" Bill asked.

"She's not here. Her mom thinks she went to the Hole."

"Then I guess that's where you're going."

"Me? Are you not coming with?"

Bill scoffed and said, "There's a reason MPD don't drink there, West. Your father won't serve us and we don't want to patronize his business. Cops try not to drink in their own jurisdictions."

I rolled my eyes. "I don't get it, why do you hate my dad so much?"

Bill grumbled a bit, like he didn't know if he wanted to share any details with me, but then said, "Because I knew him back when your mom was alive. He might come off as low-key and mellow these days, but that man was a monster once upon a time. Kind of like you."

"Not all monsters are evil," I told him. Vince crossed my mind, what he did to Fletch. It was a shockingly violent act, but it was completely justified. Vince was a good man, but he was capable of horrific things. He was good, but he was capable of doing bad things in the name of that good.

"I think society needs monsters. You need people with the devil in them to take care of the really evil fucks."

"If you say so," Bill mumbled as he drove off.

As the car rolled through the streets, I looked at the man and thought back to the first time he arrested me. It was a couple years back. My mind was in a bad way and my body was set on self-destruction.

I sat at a picnic table on the patio at the Hole with Izzy and Clyde, drinking and smoking and carrying on. It was close to the most drunk I had ever been. As I went to go put out my cigarette, I said with slurred speech, "Hey, you wanna see something cool?"

Clyde grinned as he tried to guess what I was driving at. "What, the dollar trick? Where you hold a hundred dollar bill to your arm and try to burn through Benjamin's eye?"

"Fuck the hundred," I replied. Immediately, I pressed the burning end of the cigarette against my forearm.

Izzy yelled, "Jesus Christ, West!" and tried to grab it from me, but I moved quick enough to evade her. Clyde laughed it off.

Once the cigarette was out, I said, "Wanna see me do it again?"

Clyde grinned and said, "Nobody wants to see that, West."

Ignoring him, I took out another cigarette, lit it, and put it out on my arm again. "Doesn't hurt."

Clyde said, "Alright, we get it, tough guy. Now quit fuckin' burning yourself, people are looking at you funny."

I didn't care. I lit another one and did it again.

"Jesus Christ…" Clyde muttered as he scratched the back of his head. Izzy got up and went inside as I smoked another cigarette, and put that one out on my arm, too. I must have done it five or six times.

Izzy came back through the door and my father stepped out with her, holding a fork in his hand. "The fuck are you doing, West?" he asked.

"Just having a little fun," I replied as I walked over to him. "What's the fork for?"

"It's from the kitchen," Jim told me. "Izzy said you like burning yourself. I just set this fork on the flat top on high for six minutes. You really like to burn yourself?"

"Try me." I held out my forearm. My dad took a breath then sighed and pressed the fork against my skin. I laughed as it burned through the first layer or so, leaving a large burn and dead skin in its wake. Apparently he was trying to dissuade me but I took it as a challenge. Disappointed, my father wordlessly walked back inside.

As I sat back down at the table, Clyde shook his head and Izzy gave me concerned glances. Either unaware or unconcerned, I went on. "You know," I began, "I don't think I've been hit in the face enough in my life."

"You sure about that?" Clyde asked.

"I mean, everybody needs to get clocked a few times. Right?"

"Sure, West. Whatever you say."

I thought about it for a moment, then said, "Hit me."

"What?" Clyde choked on his drink.

"Punch me in the face."

"You want me to *punch* you…in the face?"

"That's what I said, isn't it?"

Clyde and Izzy exchanged glances, then Clyde said, "Alright, but not right here. We gotta go out the gate so it's not on Hole grounds."

Excitedly, I clapped my hands together and yelled, "Al-fucking-right!" We got up and I followed Clyde out through the gate back to the alley behind the bar. One of the regulars, an older man named Red, stood out there smoking a cigarette.

I limbered up, shook my hands and my head, then braced myself. "Alright, do it," I said.

"You sure you want me to do this?" Clyde asked once more.

"Hell yeah, man, I'm ready for it."

"In the face?"

"Right here," I patted my cheek. Clyde sighed, then raised his fists and threw one across my jaw. My head snapped to the side and then back. Dazed, I touched my cheek. It hurt. Then, I grabbed Clyde in a hug, laughed and yelled, "Fucking thank you, man!"

Red stood there in disbelief at what he just witnessed and said, "What in the name of fuck was that?"

The bar cleared out a little after that and I was the last one to leave. Before I left, my father pulled me to the side. "Listen, West," he started. "This shit that went on tonight? What the fuck was all that? You know, I had people walking up to me and saying, 'man, I hope he fixes himself, whatever's wrong with him. I hope he changes.' But you know what I think? I don't think you're gonna change. I don't think you *want* to change. And that's the problem." I was silent as I listened. My father then sighed and said, "Be careful walking home, okay?"

I didn't say a word to him as I left the bar. But I felt the unbearable weight of my own fucking problems – heartbreak, alcoholism, directionlessness. And as I got back to my house, I felt sick of it. I wanted it all to just stop. So I got in my car and I drove.

Hammered beyond fucking belief, I flew down some back country roads while the music blared in my ears. I must have been going nearly a hundred miles an hour when I hit a sharp curve in the road. My car lurched to the side as I jerked the steering wheel and sailed off the road, plowing through a couple hundred feet of a cornfield and breaking through on the other side. The damage my car took was extensive. It was a real shame, too, because I fucking loved that car – a red 2000 Monte Carlo. Shards of plastic littered the ground from the shattered headlights. Shaken and weary from the experience, I pulled to a stop a couple hundred feet up the road and sat there in my car until I fell asleep. By nine in the morning I was being woken up by Bill knocking on my window.

"You alive in there?" he asked.

I looked around, hungover to piss and sore from sleeping upright. Then I noticed the cop. With a sigh, I threw my head back into the seat and rolled down the window. "Morning, Officer."

"You wanna tell me what happened here?"

"I drove through a cornfield last night," I admitted. "I was going a little too fast and couldn't turn around the bend in time."

Bill looked around, surveying the damage. "You wanna go ahead and step out of the car?"

I complied and stood there as the sunlight dazzled my eyes. Bill and I had met once when I was fifteen, when he issued me with a misdemeanor for fighting in school – disorderly conduct, I was lucky it wasn't assault considering the other kid didn't even fight back, I just knocked the fuck out of him repeatedly. "Jesus," I murmured, looking at my ruined car. "There's still corn in my undercarriage." I couldn't help but chuckle.

"You have anything to drink last night?"

"A couple beers," I half admitted, half lied. Truthfully I had drank the entire bar. But for some reason I felt compelled to tell him that alcohol was involved. Maybe it was a cry for help.

Bill sighed as if he was disappointed I told the truth. "Alright. Well," he looked around again, "I am *going* to have to arrest you. You understand that, right?"

"Yeah, I figured."

Bill scratched his head. "I'm not even sure what to charge you with exactly. I think the code is 'agricultural vandalism.'"

"I didn't even know that was a thing."

"That's because most people don't do it. Turn around for me." Bill frisked me then put me in cuffs and set me in the passenger seat of his cruiser.

"Can I ask you something?" I said after a few minutes of driving.

"Sure."

"Does it bug you when people drive really slowly in front of you? You know, because everybody's afraid of being pulled over?"

Bill let out a laugh and said, "Like you wouldn't believe." As we approached the station, he said, "Look, you seem like a smart kid. You should stay out of trouble. Get some discipline. You don't have to live like this."

My head leaned against the window. "Maybe I do."

I expected them to throw the book at me since I admitted alcohol was involved, but when I got out of booking and read the police report, Bill had left out my admission of guilt – drinking wasn't mentioned even a single time. I never understood why. The incident became a running joke in town for a while – it was a pretty fucking funny way to get arrested. But I didn't usually tell people what actually happened.

As Bill and I drove to the Hole in the Ground, I looked at him and said, "Why didn't you report that I had been drinking when you arrested me the first time a few years ago?"

Bill grumbled and replied, "Because I thought you deserved a second chance. Maybe I was wrong about that, maybe I was right. I think you have yet to prove me right, though."

I thought about his words for a second, then said, "I never told you why I did it."

He looked at me with a cocked eyebrow. "I thought it was an accident?"

"It wasn't. I was trying to flip my car," I told him. "I was trying to kill myself."

Bill looked at me, unsure how to respond, then turned his eyes forward again. "Jesus."

"That same week, not three or four days later, I met Kayla. And I was so glad that my car didn't flip." Bill choked subtly as I mentioned Kayla's name. I studied his face for a moment, then told him, "For all of the problems me and her had, I don't regret the time we had for even one second. I just wanted you to know that."

Finally, we arrived at the Hole. There was nothing left to do but face the music. Bill looked at me and said, "Good luck. Call me if you find anything out."

"Will do." With that, I got out of the car and stood in front of the steps of the bar, staring at the spot where Kayla and I first spoke to each other.

There was nothing left to do but go inside.

Chapter 18

My muscles were tense as I stepped through the door. It was almost like a hush fell over the bar as I stepped into the pool room. Nobody said anything, they just stopped what they were doing for a moment and stared goddamn daggers at me.

"As you were," I mumbled with a wave of my hand and walked through to the bar. I could see the bullet holes in the walls, and the one that almost hit Izzy. Guilt coursed through my veins as I relived that night. But I wasn't going to let myself dwell on it.

I walked up to the bar. Jane was working – my father was nowhere to be found. I was thankful for that. There wasn't enough preparation in the world to face that music. While I looked around the bar, scanning for Kimmy and waiting for Jane to come down to me, Clyde walked past my back. He yelled, "Whoa, careful everybody! The rapist is here! Watch your drinks, hide yo' wife!"

It took restraint that I didn't know I had but I bit my tongue and kept my mouth shut. I knew he didn't actually believe that, but he was pissed and it was a good way to get under my skin. As I glanced around, I noticed Izzy sitting at the end of the bar. She looked at me, then quickly looked away. Kimmy sat down at the other end next to Dane and Matilda. I wasn't ready for any of it.

Jane came over with a look of surprise, like she was shocked to see me. "Holy shit, West. Where did you disappear to? Nobody's seen you in like three or four days."

"I had to go take care of some things," I replied vaguely. I wasn't exactly keen on telling people I just got out of the psych ward.

"Did you hear about what happened?" Jane asked, almost eagerly.

"You're gonna have to be a lot more specific, Jane."

"Somebody shot up the bar!" she exclaimed.

My eyebrows raised in feigned surprise. "Oh yeah?"

"It was the night of Kayla's funeral. Apparently someone broke in or something, stole your dad's handgun and shot a bunch of holes in the walls. By the time the cops got here the bar was empty."

"They have any idea who did it?" Christ I wanted a drink.

"The security camera's been broken for months," Jane said, "and nobody's come forward with any information on it, so as far as I know any theories are dead in the water." She paused as if she expected me to say something, then leaned in a little and said, "Was it you? That's what your dad thinks."

"No," I lied. "He really thinks it was me?"

"Oh yeah," Jane nodded. "He was in rage mode the other day. Whoever it was, they better hope Jim doesn't find out. I don't think he's gonna call the cops when he finds them. I think he's gonna eighty-six them himself."

"Wow," I replied, trying to hide my nerves. "I leave for a couple days and all hell breaks loose."

"Hell tends to still break loose when you're here," Jane laughed.

"True."

"You drinking? Jack and coke?"

My mouth tried to say no, but instead the words that came out were, "Eh... I'll just have a Miller Lite."

"Gross," Jane teased, then walked over to the taps. I subtly looked at the reflection of the small crowd in the mirror behind the taps and the liquor shelf. She set the cold beer down in front of me. "Enjoy."

For a long time, I stared at it. Maybe I could learn moderation. I had tried and failed before, but maybe I really could learn to drink responsibly. Just have a couple of beers, nothing crazy. Maybe have some mixed drinks or a bit of liquor as long as I wasn't driving. Maybe I could do that. But I wanted to be sober. I wanted to get my life in order, clear my name, find Kayla's murderer. I wanted to make up to Izzy, patch things up with Clyde. But most of all, I realized, I wanted to not be sober. As I picked up the glass and held it to my lips, I heard a voice come from beside me.

"What are you doing, West?" Izzy asked. She looked at me with utter disappointment.

"Just...something to take the edge off," I replied with quiet shame.

"You said you wanted to be sober. So do it. If you drink that, then you're just undoing whatever progress you made when you were gone." Before I could even answer, she was gone.

I looked at the glass in my hand. Izzy was right. If I drank it, then I would have been right back where I started, and by the end of the night I would be so fucking wasted that I wouldn't know where I was when I woke up.

So I set the glass back down on the table and walked out back to smoke a cigarette while I figured out what I would say to Kimmy. Clyde stood towards the back smoking one of his own. Maybe I could talk to him.

"Hey," I said as I walked over. "Can we talk?"

"What do you want?" he asked curtly, biting back his anger.

"You want me to stop hooking up with Izzy, right?"

Clyde shot me a bewildered look. "I don't give a fuck what you do, West. I wasn't even that mad that you slept with her. I'm mad that you fucking lied about it. You lied right to my fucking face. So no, I don't give a fuck if you hook up with her. Don't fucking talk to me." Angrily, he tossed his cigarette and walked off. Alone, I stood on the patio, wondering if there would ever be reconciliation. But there were no more distractions, I realized. So I went inside and walked over to Kimmy, Dane, and Matilda.

"Hey," I began. "We need to talk."

Dane replied first, "About what?"

"I need to talk to *Kimmy*."

Matilda spoke next. "Whatever you have to say to her, you can say in front of us. We're not leaving you alone with anybody."

The pure indignance I felt was something I didn't know how to grasp, but I couldn't lash out. I needed to stay in control of myself. "Fine, then so be it." I looked directly at Kimmy and said, "Fletch told me you're the one who started the rumors. The ones about me being a rapist."

Kimmy shot a glance at Matilda and Dane then said, "I have no idea what you're talking about."

"Bullshit. Fletch was a lot of things, but I always knew when he was lying. He wasn't lying about that. You started the rumors and I need to know why."

Kimmy resisted again. "I told you I don't know, West."

"Fine," I replied. "Why don't I tell you what I think happened?" The three of them glanced at each other with doubt, then returned their attention to me. "I think that someone at Black Rock actually did roofie you and Matilda. I believe that that happened and it's fortunate nothing worse came of it. But I think that night at the tavern, Dane saw me and Matilda talking and he wanted to nip it in the bud. So when you all started talking about the roofie incident, Dane suggested or implied that I might have been the one who did it, and you two convinced yourselves that was the case. Then somebody you told had it out for Kayla – whether it was a fixation or a vendetta, I don't know – but they called the bars and posed as a cop so they could set me up for when they killed her. How's that sound, am I in the ballpark?"

Kimmy looked at the other two, then finally said quietly, "There's more...."

"More?" I asked. "Like what?"

"I can't tell you that," Kimmy said. "But I will say this: it has something to do with when Kayla was mugged."

I furrowed my brow in confusion. "What does that have to do with anything?"

Before Kimmy could answer, Matilda squeezed her arm, signaling her to stop. "Sorry, West. I can't tell you. Kayla told me not to." Then, as I stood there baffled, the trio got up and walked through the bar to the back door. What in the hell was she talking about? The mugging happened months ago. Was she implying the person who robbed Kayla was the same person who made the phone calls? Why the fuck would those events be connected.

As I racked my brain, I realized how fuzzy the alcohol had made my timeline. For a visual aid, I pulled up my phone's calendar. As my eyes scanned over the dates, trying to piece together the series of events, my low battery signal popped on the screen. "Fuck me," I muttered to myself. I went back to the kitchen and plugged my phone into the charger on the wall.

And then it hit me.

The night Kayla was mugged, she said she had to go to the Hole to grab her phone charger.

Her phone charger was the one plugged into the wall.

She had never been back to the bar after that night.

Maybe if I hadn't been intoxicated so much of the time, I would have realized the obvious thing staring me in the face: Kayla never got her charger.

It was like a bomb went off in my head as my ears started ringing and I suddenly realized I knew less of the truth than I thought I did. Quickly, I snatched the charger out of its socket, burst through the back door, and walked up to Kimmy. "Kayla said she went to the Hole that night to get her charger. Then why is it still here?" I held the charger up to Kimmy's face. "She never got mugged, did she?" Kimmy didn't budge, but she looked like she was going to any moment. I tried a different approach. "Look, Kimmy... I'm sorry about what happened to Fletch. You know that I know how bad it hurts better than damn near anybody else. Nobody should have to go through that kind of loss. But if you don't tell me the truth right now, somebody will have died for nothing, and the person who did it won't ever be caught. So please, Kimmy, tell me: Kayla never got mugged that night, did she?"

Kimmy looked between me and the item in my hand for a moment, then finally broke. "No," she said. "Kayla never got mugged."

"Then what happened?" I demanded, struggling not to raise my voice. Dane and Matilda stood by silently. As Kimmy seemed to debate whether or not to tell me, Bill's advice ran through my head. *You've got to make them feel pressured yet comforted.* With a deep breath, I said, "Look, Kimmy... If you know something, anything at all, that might be important – eventually the cat's gonna be out of the bag. And I know you don't trust me, and you have no reason to, but when push comes to shove... Well, the police are gonna be pretty interested in what you know, too."

That seemed to do the trick. Kimmy finally spoke candidly. "I don't know if you can handle this, West."

"Handle what?"

"What happened...."

My gut tightened in a knot. Part of me knew what was coming, I think. A part of me knew back when it happened, too. But I never wanted to believe it. "Please," I said softly. "You have to tell me."

Kimmy bit her lip, like trying to stop herself from speaking, then she finally said it: "Kayla wasn't robbed that night..."

The three or four seconds that passed between that sentence and the next one could have been an eternity.

"She was raped."

The world could have ended right there from the pain that I felt hearing those words. My voice was silent but inside I was screaming. Inside I was pounding my knuckles into the concrete until they bled. Inside the world was on fire. But on the outside, I just stood there, unable to speak.

"And we thought you did it," Kimmy added.

"Why?" I muttered weakly.

Kimmy looked at Dane and Matilda, then back to me. "The same reason Kayla warned me about it," she said. "Because it happened here."

Chapter 19

I never wanted a drink so fucking badly in my life.

It was after three in the morning and I still sat in my apartment, wide awake. The revelation that Kayla had been raped was more than I could handle. At least I got to be drunk when I found out she died – this was something different. Kayla had to live through that experience, and live with the memory of it happening. Where was I when it happened? Getting piss drunk in a ditch somewhere. It was my job to protect her and provide for her and now I knew I failed at both of those things.

I wanted to breathe fire, scream my rage and fury up to God until he went deaf from hearing it. I wanted to burn Matchstick to the fucking ground and walk through its ashes. I wanted to die. I wanted to drink. I wanted something.

I beat my fist into the wall until it cracked and my knuckles bled. Then I turned and slammed my fist into the refrigerator, leaving a dent where my knuckles had hit it. Pain wasn't enough to soothe me. And there would never be anything I could do to make it right. I could never tell Kayla that it would be okay – it wouldn't ever be okay. She was dead and I failed her. I wished I were dead too.

The gun still sitting in my car popped into my head. It would have been so easy. There was one bullet left, still chambered in the cylinder. All it would take was a little pressure from my finger and boom – life over. No more pain. No more thoughts. No more memories.

But what would I leave behind? A slumped body leaning forward in the driver's seat for my friends to find?

No. I couldn't do that. All I could do was try and bear it.

For hours, I tossed and turned, desperately wishing I could sleep, wishing Izzy were there, wishing Kayla were there. I had never known pain until I had to deal with it alone and sober. Suddenly, I remembered I still had a bottle of jack in my cupboard. In a fit, I ran over and pulled it from its resting place and quickly took the cap off, then put the bottle to my lips.

But just as it touched my tongue, I lurched forward and spit it back into the sink. The bottle emptied as I poured it down the drain.

Alcohol couldn't be my solution, not again. I would have to deal with it in sobriety or not at all. And for the first time in a very long time, I let myself feel. It was the most painful thing I had ever experienced in my life – it was easy to run, but harder to stand.

The daylight hours finally began to roll in, and with my brain no closer to being able to sleep, I buckled and took a Seroquel in the hopes that it would knock me out. I thought about taking several to see how high they would get me, but I pushed those thoughts back and only took the one. It didn't take long for the pill to kick in and soon I finally began to pass out. But just before I fell asleep, my phone buzzed with a Facebook message notification. Fighting to stay conscious, I looked at it.

It was from Kayla's friend Robin.

"*Hey, Kimmy told me she told you about what happened... Can we talk?*"

Before I could respond, I fell asleep.

***

I remembered the first "date" Kayla and I had. It wasn't a date, really. I just went over to her apartment. Not even in a hang out and fuck kind of way – I thought it would just be a platonic thing.

Nervously and anxiously, I watched the clock at work. My father was there with me. He asked with a bit of a chuckle, "What's got you so fidgety?"

"Nothing," I said. "I'm seeing this girl tonight."

"Oh yeah? What's her name?"

"Kayla. She's been in here a couple of times, you've probably seen her before."

"Is it a date?"

"I don't think so," I told him. "I'm going over to her place. She specifically said, and I quote, 'you can't spend the night and we're not having sex.'"

My father laughed. "Well I guess it's good to set the expectations. When are you seeing her?"

"I told her I'd come over as soon as I got off."

He nodded toward the door. "Then get out of here," he said. "I'll close the bar."

"Really?" I asked excitedly. "You sure?"

"Of course. You owe me one."

"Thank you, thank you!" I cheered, then ran out the door, hopped in my car, and drove to Kayla's place. It was the first time I had ever been there. She greeted me at the door dressed in a black hoodie that said "I'm a cat," in white letters and black jeans – definitely not the outfit of a woman trying to seduce somebody.

"Hey!" she said brightly as she opened the door. "Can you help me with something?"

"Um, sure?" I replied, taken aback.

"Sorry, I was moving this desk I just got and it would be a *lot* easier with two people."

"Well I certainly hope this isn't why you invited me over," I laughed. Kayla laughed too.

"No, no, I promise. I just thought I would have more time." She led the way upstairs and I followed her, trying hard to not stare too closely at her ass as she walked. She showed me to the room with the desk – still in a box, unopened. "Okay," she started, "I need to get it from *this* room to my bedroom." She went in to pick up one side of it, but I shooed her away and picked it up myself. "Okay, muscles," Kayla giggled.

"What can I say," I replied. "I've gotta be good for something, right?"

After I got the desk situated, we went downstairs to her living room. A very small hairless cat darted by. "What the fuck was that?" I asked.

Kayla laughed and said, "That's my kitty. I call her Yoder because she looks like a derpy little Yoda." She knelt down and the cat hesitantly went to her, probably a little put off by my presence. The cat was cute in an ugly sort of way, but it clung onto Kayla like a baby does its mother.

"Hi, Yoder," I said, holding a hand out for the little cat to sniff. Kayla made us a couple of screwdrivers and we sat on the sofa. The cat had its freedom to roam, but it crawled right up to me and sat in my lap.

"Wow," Kayla said. "She loves you! She never likes people, I didn't think she would even come out."

"What can I say? I have a way with the ladies."

Kayla laughed and sat close to me. "Movie or music?"

"That depends," I said. "What music do you have?"

"You like Pink Floyd?" she asked me.

"Does anybody not?"

"Right?" she giggled. "Hang on, I've got something." She hopped up and grabbed a DVD, put it in the player, then let it run.

"What's this?" I asked as Kayla flopped down beside me, even closer than she had been before.

"It's a Pink Floyd concert, *Pulse*. It's one of my favorites."

The concert began to play on TV and we watched and listened, enraptured by the music. With every song, we inched closer together, until *Brain Damage* began to play. Kayla looked at me and said, "You know, just because I said we're not having sex doesn't mean you can't kiss me."

I looked at her and smiled, then, as the chorus began to play, I leaned in and delivered the greatest kiss of my life. The music swelled, it was passionate and sweet and perfect. There was doubt in my mind that no other kiss I would ever have would come close. We slept together that night and I didn't leave until the next morning. The rest would be history.

Anymore it feels like the only place we can ever find each other is on the dark side of the moon.

A year later we would have a very different kind of night.

"I'm not gaslighting you, you're just wrong!" I shouted as we sat in Kayla's bed at four in the morning. I was drunk and she wasn't.

"I never said that!" she argued. "I know I didn't say that!"

I pulled out my phone and scrolled through our messages until I found the one I was looking for. "Yes you did! It's right here!"

Kayla didn't look at the phone, just rolled over and said, "It's four in the morning, I'm going to sleep, West!"

"No!" I shouted. "You can't just fucking shut down in the middle of an argument! Just admit that you were wrong! Just admit it!"

Suddenly, Kayla screamed and rolled over, then flung herself on top of me and smacked the phone out of my hand. In an instant, her hands were on my throat holding me down. After half a minute of her gripping my throat hard enough to block the air but not hard enough to hurt, I threw her off of me and she hit the floor.

As I sat up, I yelled, "What the fuck was that!"

"Just go away!" Kayla cried out as she began to sob. "Get out of here! Just go, please!"

"You just fucking strangled me!"

"Just go!" She got up and ran to another room. I followed her. I didn't know why and I still don't, but I followed her to every room she went to as she sobbed. At some point that night, I fell asleep. Maybe Kayla slept, maybe she didn't. All I remembered was drinking every drop of liquor in that house and passing out as the sun came up. She got me out of bed around noon the next day. "You should go."

My head killed me as I sat up and remembered what happened the night before. That was the moment when things were irreparably broken. I told her it was her fault, *she* was the one who choked *me*. And that was true – but the reality was I knew what I was fucking doing. I pushed her and I pushed her until she broke. She had already cheated on me by that point and even though I told her I had forgiven her, I hated her for it. I wanted her to break. It didn't even hurt when she choked me, but I played it up like I was the victim of domestic violence when I knew goddamn well that I wasn't. But I could read the writing on the wall. I picked up Yoder and held the small cat, standing in the kitchen, trying to warm her heart through brute force by making her associate her cat's happiness with me. Kayla looked at me and said, "That won't work anymore."

We couldn't stay away from each other, though. We got back together and broke up a few more times after that. And as I awoke with the text from Robin the day after finding out Kayla had been raped, I thought maybe we should have ended things that night after all. Robin said, *"Can you meet me at the trail today?"*

It was a little after noon when I woke up and texted back: *"Yes."*

Chapter 20

Nervously, I walked from my apartment to the trail, the one right across from the Hole, around six in the evening – the earliest Robin could meet me. I didn't know what Robin could possibly tell me that could fuck me up more than the revelation from the night before, and I wasn't ready to find out. But that was all I could do.

When I stepped out of my apartment, my neighbor was standing outside on the sidewalk several feet away from her door as bees carelessly buzzed around it. She stood there staring at it with her arms crossed and I couldn't figure out why.

"You alright?" I asked.

"Yeah," she said. "Just wish I could go inside."

"You lock yourself out?"

"No," she said softly. Then she gestured toward the bees. "Freaking bees."

"Oh," I said, noticing them buzzing around. "Yeah, bees scare the shit out of me, too."

"I'm allergic," she said.

"Oh, shit," I remarked as I suddenly realized why she was standing there. I thought about just walking away, but I didn't. Instead, I said, "Wait here," then ran back into my apartment for a second and returned with a black denim jacket. "Alright," I said, "let's try something." I walked over to her and held the jacket around her, hovering it a few inches over her head and torso. "Walk with me," I said.

Quickly, we walked the short way to her door and I stood there calmly as bees swarmed me despite how nervous they made me, keeping her protected beneath the jacket. After a second, she got her door unlocked and opened, ran inside, and yelled, "Thank you!" as the door swung shut.

Carelessly, I tossed the jacket back into my apartment and began my walk to the trail. I didn't know why I had helped her, but I was glad that I did.

As I walked, I desperately wished I could take a shot or have a few hits of some grass, but forcefully I pushed those thoughts from my mind. For the first time in my adult life, my head was clear, and so many things began to make sense.

Robin was sitting on a bench by a small cafe. It was funny, I realized; I had been going to the Hole for years and years but not once had I ever set foot into the cafe directly across the street from it. I guess if they served Jameson I might have gone.

"Hey," Robin said with a small wave as I approached. She was a beautiful young woman with dark blonde hair and a figure sculpted from an hourglass. Drunkenly, I had made a pass at her a few times to piss off Kayla, but Robin never seemed to hold it against me. She was a good woman. Kayla's life had always been better off for having Robin in it – something that couldn't be said for me.

"Hey," I replied as I pulled out a cigarette and struck a match. I handed it to Robin.

"Thanks," she said, taking it from me. I pulled out another one and lit it for myself. Anxiously, I took a seat next to her as the sun beat down on us, brightly shining even through my sunglasses. It was hotter than hell, but I didn't mind the heat.

Robin took a drag from her cigarette and stared across the bar at the street. I wanted to say something, but I figured she would start talking when she was ready. Finally, she began to speak. "I hate that bar."

I looked at her for a moment then turned my head toward the Hole. "Yeah, me too."

Robin took another drag and said, "So what did Kimmy tell you?"

My gut tightened. I didn't want to have to think about it. "She told me that Kayla was actually raped that night she was robbed. She said it happened at the Hole. I don't know if she meant in the parking lot or if she means someone followed Kayla inside. But that's what she told me."

Robin mulled over my words for a moment. "That's not entirely the truth," she said vaguely.

"Then what is the entire truth?" I asked. My gut tightened into an even harder knot. I could have been sick.

Robin frowned and said, "Just... if I tell you, promise me you won't get mad."

"I can't promise that, Robin," I told her truthfully. "But what I *can* promise is I won't act out. I'm not that guy anymore. At least, I hope that I'm not."

"I always thought you were a good man," she said, "even when you were at your worst. I wish you and Kayla had been able to work through your differences, but...." She trailed off.

"Hardly matters now," I said.

Robin sighed and said, "Did anything seem off about Kayla to you? In the last couple months that you were dating, I mean."

I thought about it for a second and said, "Not really. I mean, I wasn't paying that much attention. I was preoccupied with getting plastered and barely holding my shit together." Robin frowned again. I asked, "Why? What was going on?"

"Kayla was seeing somebody," she said. "Somebody else, behind your back."

"*What?*" I asked sharply.

"I'm sorry nobody told you," Robin went on, "but we didn't want to put you through any more trouble than you were already going through. And Kayla thought you might freak out and lose your shit if you found out."

I didn't know what to say. I simply stammered for a second. But after I thought about it, I couldn't say it didn't make sense. "It's okay," I told her. "You did what any good friend would do. When you say 'we,' who does that include? Who else knew about it?"

"Just me, Kayla, and the guy she was seeing," Robin explained. "What happened that night is that she met him at the Hole to try and break things off. He didn't take it very well, and then he…" Robin couldn't finish the sentence. "You know the rest."

My mind couldn't quite comprehend what I was hearing. "She told me she went to the police… Was that true?"

Robin shook her head. "No."

"Well why the hell didn't she?" I asked.

"She was afraid of him," Robin told me.

Suddenly it clicked. "Is that why she was going to North Carolina?"

Robin nodded. "Yeah. She wanted to get as far away from him as possible."

My heart hurt for her, for my own failure to protect her. I should have been livid about the affair. I should have burned Matchstick to the ground. But I didn't want to. The fact that she cheated on me hardly mattered now. All that mattered was the truth. "Did she ever tell you who it was?"

"No," Robin said. I believed her. At that point, if she had known anything about it, she would have said something. "But I do know one thing."

"What?"

"He works at the Hole."

"What…?" I mumbled in shock. "He…works there?"

Robin nodded again. "That's all that I know. She kept everything else to herself. But I would bet you anything that the guy she was seeing, that's the one who killed her." Robin finished her cigarette, rolled the remaining tobacco out of the cigarette butt, then tucked it in her purse to throw away later. She rose to her feet and I followed suit, and before she walked away, she said, "I'm really sorry, West," and put her arms around me.

"Thank you," I said, still in a daze as I returned her embrace. As Robin walked away, I stood there thinking about everything she had just told me. Kayla had been cheating on me with one of my coworkers, and there was only one person who made any kind of sense. The guy who pulled more tail than me, that nearly every stray that walked through that bar had fucked at some point. A guy with violent tendencies that could be capable of anything, and who would have reason to try and get back on me if he had his own suspicions about my devious behavior.

The only person that made sense to me was Clyde. It had to be him.

As I reached that answer, my phone rang. It was Officer Sparks. "Hey," I said, "it's kind of a bad time."

"*Well, you're not gonna have too many more good times to talk,*" Bill said through the phone.

"What do you mean?"

"*It's too important for a phone call,*" he said. "*Can you meet me at the Black Rock Tavern tonight around ten? I'm working the graveyard shift tonight, but I'll have time to take a detour at Black Rock before I go on patrol.*"

"I guess," I replied distantly. "What for, though?"

"*I think I know who made those phone calls.*"

My eyes widened and my heart dropped. "I'll be there at ten."

***

The time passed slowly until ten at night rolled around. It was difficult to keep myself occupied without the help of substances, but I managed to do it. By the grace of God, I was staying sober.

People turned their heads and looked at me as I walked into the bar. Despite the arrested-for-rape story being provably false, people still believed it. The truth didn't matter. What mattered to them was a good story, and it was definitely a hell of a story.

Nervously, I glanced around, looking for Bill. The Black Rock Tavern was outside of the Matchstick Police Department's jurisdiction, so the MPD officers were welcome to drink there without people being wary of them. Bill was something of a regular; he would pop in a few times a month. Today had been his first day back on the job since Kayla died. After a minute of looking, I finally spotted him at the corner of the bar, sitting in uniform with a bottle of water in front of him.

"Hey," I said as I approached him.

"Hey," he said back. "I don't have a lot of time before my shift starts, but why don't you go ahead and take a seat? You're gonna want to be sitting down for this."

Anxiously and unsure of what to expect, I sat down beside him. "So who do you think made the phone call?" I asked.

Bill sucked his teeth, then turned his head and said, "Come on over." At that moment, a man I recognized approached the bar.

It was Neil, the man who had first told me of the things people had been saying. "Hey," he said quietly, almost like he was defeated.

"What the fuck…?" was all I could get out. I almost jumped up to accost him, but Bill waved me down with his hand.

"Hey, hey," he said gruffly. "Be civil."

"Are you the one who made the phone calls?" I asked directly.

After a moment, Neil said plainly, "Yeah."

I looked at Bill. "So are you gonna arrest him or do I have to get some more cops down here?"

"Hear him out," Bill said. "Look, as soon as you said 'Neil' the other day, I had a suspicion about what had happened. So I asked him about it. And I was right."

Confused and frustrated, I looked at Neil. "So why don't you go ahead and fill me in?"

Neil sighed and said, "Look, man... What I told you that night was true – at least, that's what I had been told. Kimmy, Dane and all them... They all told me they were *positive* you were a bad guy, that you hurt women and did fucking terrible things to them. But none of them were gonna do anything about it. They just kept their drinks away from you and told the girls to stay away." Neil ran his fingers through his hair as he continued to confess. I could see the guilt in his eyes as he told me what happened. "So that's why I confronted you. I thought, *man, is this guy really doing all that and nobody's even gonna say anything? Somebody's gotta do something*. I thought just tellin' you what was going on would be enough, but then I kept hearing about you at all these bars. I got scared, man. I've got a daughter about your age. I've got a wife. They come out to these places. The thought of them getting hurt... I wasn't gonna let that happen. So I did what I thought I had to do."

Part of me couldn't believe what I was hearing. The other part of me couldn't believe I was agreeing with him. Bill spoke before I could. "Neil had been asking me about what kind of charges someone like that would get, so I told him. Gave him all the official terminology and everything, didn't think twice about it. I didn't know that's what he was gonna do with the information. But Neil's been a friend of mine for a long time, West. He didn't hurt anybody. The only person he's hurt is you and your reputation."

Neil said, "I'm sorry for what I did. But I'm not sorry that I did it. If the shoe were on the other foot, I'd hope you would do the same thing to me."

I thought it over for a while, barely able to comprehend what I was being told. Finally, after a minute, I said, "You're right. I would have done the same thing. Maybe not posed as a cop, but I would have done something. And for what it's worth… I forgive you for it. I don't think you're a bad person. I think you were misguided and just doing what you thought was best."

Neil breathed a sigh of relief and held his hand out to mine. I shook it. "Thank you," he said.

Bill looked at him and asked, "Could you give us a moment, Neil?"

"Sure thing, Bill." With that, Neil got up and walked away.

Once Neil was out of ear shot, Bill said, "So we know the phone call and the murder aren't connected."

"For what it's worth, I think I figured out who did it," I told him. I was still uneasy about my conclusion. I couldn't picture Clyde doing that. Honestly, it sounded more like something that I would do than him.

"Well," Bill said with a groan. Whatever was coming next wasn't going to be good. "I don't think it's gonna be worth much."

"Why?" I asked quizzically.

Bill sighed and said, "I don't know how to tell you this, West, but the detective in charge of the investigation..."

"Yeah?"

"He's going to charge you for the murder. Tomorrow."

"*What*?!" I exclaimed loudly.

Bill shook his head and said, "They determined Kayla most likely lost her life inside the bar. You're the only person that they know was there that night – you made that pretty damn certain when you kicked everyone else out. You blacked out, woke up and the bar was a chaotic disaster. You woke up thirty feet away from Kayla's body." Bill choked as he said her name, but stoically pushed it back down. "Regardless of whether you did it or not, it looks like you two had a fight, she left and came back, you were drunk, attacked her in the bar and took her life in the process. Then you tried to hide the body in the dumpster. That's the narrative the detective is building."

My mouth hung agape. "But... But I didn't...."

"That doesn't really matter, West. All that matters is what you can prove." Bill sighed again and said, "I'll do what I can for you, but you need to come to terms with the fact that tonight might be your last night of freedom."

Stunned. Shocked. Baffled. Terrified. Those were the only words that came to mind. Without saying a thing, I rose from my seat and walked out of the tavern.

As I drove away, I wasn't sure where I was going at first. But instinctively, my hands and feet took me to the only home I knew.

I went to the Hole.
I needed to see my father.

Chapter 21

My car idled in the parking lot of the Hole in the Ground as I burned through cigarettes. My father was working, but I didn't want to go in there until the bar had cleared out. I couldn't face people at that moment. Maybe I would never see most of them again. The only person I really wanted to see was Izzy, but that bridge had been burned to the ground, I felt. My only shot at freedom was the hope that my father still had a good lawyer on speed dial.

My mind drifted back to Izzy. I remembered holding her in my arms as we laid in bed. "I feel safe with you," she told me. I gently kissed the top of her head.

"You are," I said to her.

There were a lot of things I could have regretted in life; my entire twenty-six years on earth at that point could have been regrets. There were people I had hurt, people I lied to, people I fucked and fucked over. But I didn't regret any of that. My only real regret was that I could never keep myself from going back to Kayla. I had been in love with Izzy for a long time, but the thought of losing Kayla to another man drove me to wild fury. I couldn't let it go. I needed to have Kayla just so nobody else could, so I would go back to Kayla and drop Izzy. Drop her over and over again. And because of that, I had ruined the best thing that ever happened to me – her.

The last car in the parking lot that wasn't my own finally left. There was only one cigarette left in my pack. As I lit it, I wondered if it would be the last one I would ever have.

Without me even thinking about it, my hand reached into my pocket, pulled out my phone, and called Izzy. It went to voicemail – something I had expected. I didn't even know what I would say, but I just began to talk.

"Hey... I don't really know how to say this, but... I think shit is about to hit the fan. I might not be around for a while. I'm about to go into the Hole and see my father. I just wanted you to know a few things first. You're amazing. You're smart, you're an incredible artist, you're hilarious. You're sensitive. You like almost all the same things that I do and we're so in sync. You don't judge me for my mistakes the same way as everyone else does. And I just melt every time that I see you. I was right the first time I said it. I'm in love with you – for better or worse, I'm in love with you. There's no way to shape it any differently and that's that. I'm in love with you, Izzy. I have been for a long time. With me that means a whole lot of bad news – high highs and low lows. I'm all over the map right now and I feel like I can barely function. I don't know what we are or what I want us to be, and I'm sorry for the way that I am. All that matters to me right now is that you'll still be my friend at the end."

With nothing left to say, nothing left to do, I hung up the phone and flicked the cigarette butt out through my car window. The .38 special was still in my glovebox, so I took it out and tucked it into my belt. There was still a bullet chambered in the cylinder, I reminded myself. Then I opened the door, stepped out, and made the slow, dreadful walk up to the Hole.

My father was the only one still in the bar. He looked almost surprised to see me, but the surprise was shadowed with disappointment. "There you are," he said simply.

"Dad," I began, "we need to talk."

***

As I sat at the bar in front of the taps, I looked at myself in the mirror behind the liquor shelves. The guy looking back at me looked weary, worse for wear. He looked like shit. Blue eyes dimmed from exhaustion and a scruffy beard that desperately needed a trim. It didn't really matter, though. Nobody leaves behind a beautiful corpse.

"You hungry?" my father asked me. "I'm gonna turn on the fryers, toss in some wings."

"Not really," I said, "but have at it."

My father went into the kitchen and I heard the sound of the fryer working as he heated it up. When he came back, he poured two glasses of Macallan and slid me one.

"I'm good, actually," I told him, sliding it back.

"Since when do you turn down liquor?" he asked.

"Since I stopped drinking," I replied. For some reason, when I said it that time, it felt like it was truer than when I would say it before. It wasn't a hiatus or a break. It was permanent.

"Huh," my father breathed. "Didn't see that coming. How long has it been?"

"Since I had a drink?"

"Yeah."

I thought about it. "About a week, I think. My timeline is a little fuzzy. Everything has been so fucking crazy."

My father rounded the bar and took a seat beside me. "I get the feeling there are some things you want to tell me," he said. "Namely, where my gun went."

My face flushed with guilt. Begrudgingly, ashamedly, I pulled the pistol tucked in my belt and set it on the bar. "Yeah."

Jim looked at it but didn't touch it. Then, he looked at me and asked, "Wanna tell me what happened?"

I let out a deep breath. "I went crazy after Kayla's funeral," I told him. "After me and Clyde got into it, I thought I needed it to protect myself. God knows why. It doesn't even make sense. What was I gonna do, shoot him to death? With a stolen gun I don't have a permit for? Self-defense?" I scoffed at myself. "I don't think I would have done it," I said. "But with how fucking trashed and out of control I was getting… Maybe I would have. But I shot the gun around the bar. I almost hit Izzy."

My father shook his head and said, "After everything I've taught you about gun safety and the seriousness of violence."

"Yeah," I replied. "I guess I'm just used to learning things the hard way."

"I've come damn close to killing a few people in my lifetime," he said. "I know how it feels."

His words offered little comfort, but it was good to know he wasn't vitriolically furious at me like I imagined he would be. "I checked myself into the hospital right after, specifically the psych ward. I got away from drugs and alcohol for a few days and haven't touched it since."

"You went to the *hospital?*" he scoffed.

"Yeah...?" I said, confused by his reaction.

"All they're gonna do is put a label on you and keep you from fucking doing things because of it," he said. "You should have just come to me."

"With all due respect, dad, I think I made the right decision. Not like it matters much now, though."

"Why's that?"

I braced myself for the really hard part of the conversation. "I've learned a few things," I began. "For starters, they're gonna charge me with Kayla's murder tomorrow." I remembered it was past midnight, then said with a grimace, "Today, actually. And I also think I know who did it?"

My father eyed me curiously, as though he didn't believe me that I had an idea who the killer was. "Really? What's your theory?"

"I think it was Clyde. I mean, it almost has to have been. Kayla was cheating on me with someone who works here – Clyde is the only thing that makes sense. I think he followed her here that night and killed her for breaking things off with him, then set me up for it." Even as I told him my theory, I wasn't sure that I believed it. Something about it was off.

Jim shook his head and said, "That's a great theory, West. Maybe Clyde *was* fucking her behind your back. But he didn't kill her."

"How do you know?" I asked in bewilderment.

"You don't remember, do you?" my father said. "Clyde had a bonfire the night Kayla died. There were people at his house until almost four in the morning."

Suddenly the memory snapped back to me. Izzy had told me, right before I closed down the bar that night, that she was going to a bonfire at Clyde's. That's why my theory didn't make sense – because Clyde had a fucking alibi. He was at his own bonfire with Izzy. The only one who wasn't there was….

My father spoke again. "West, I know you don't want to hear this, but the only person who could have done it… I mean, there's only one person who could have gotten into the bar that night. There's only one person that was here. West…" He didn't want to finish his sentence, I could tell by the look on his face. "It was you."

I wanted to scream. I wanted to run. I wanted to spit the universe into a black fucking void. It couldn't have been me. Except he was right – I was the only one in the right spot, with the right amount of disinhibition, with the right motive, and with the rage of the devil to do it.

I killed Kayla.

Chapter 22

"How...How...?" I stammered, trying not to pass out from the revelation.

Jim shook his head somberly. "I'm sorry, West. I had a feeling from the beginning that it was you, but I really wanted to give you the benefit of the doubt. But we both know the truth."

"I... I loved her, though...."

"Did you?" my father asked pointedly. "You loved her body, sure. Maybe you even did actually love her at some point. But that all died the first time she cheated on you with another man. I know you, West. I've been there since the day you were born. And I know the rage that you carried around for her. Most people don't know that rage. They don't see it. But I do. You get it from me. And for that, I am sorry."

I couldn't process what I was hearing, but it made sense. Even in my shell shocked mental state, I knew that it made sense. "What am I going to do?" I asked softly.

"It'll be alright," my father told me. "I'm still in contact with a pretty solid lawyer. He might be able to help you out."

"I don't want to go to prison," I said more to myself than to him.

"There are certain realities you're going to have to face, West," he said, trying to reassure me. "Just work on remembering everything you can about the night it happened and try to find ways to spin it as justified or as a drunken accident."

"Spin it?" I repeated. "Dad, a girl is dead because of me. I can't spin that."

"Well, that's what lawyers are for. Hang tight, I've gotta make a call." He got up, took out his phone, then stepped outside with a cigarette in hand as he said, "Hey, it's Jim...."

The world swirled around me as I thought about what was going to happen. All I wanted to do was to tell Kayla I was sorry. But the closest I would ever get would be pictures. I pulled my phone from my pocket and opened up my photo gallery. For a minute, I scrolled through photographs of happier times. Every picture of us at the mountains, at the beach, at concerts, on vacation, just sitting at home. But almost every picture left a sour taste in my mouth. What the pictures didn't show were the arguments and fights that took place before and after. And almost every single one of them was punctuated with discord.

It had been so long since I heard Kayla's voice, and I just wanted to hear it again. I pulled up an old video of her, one where she didn't know I was recording her from across her bedroom. She looked especially pretty that day and I wanted to document it, so I slyly pulled my camera up on her bed and recorded her sitting in a chair, grinning at her and waiting for her to notice. But before she realized I was recording, she abruptly slapped her knee, stood up and said, "Welp, I'm gonna go blow up that bathroom." I laughed harder than I had ever laughed before when it happened, and watching the video again I still laughed through the tears welling in my eyes. I never thought I could hurt her.

Another habit I had was recording the screen when we had video calls, which we both preferred over voice only phone calls. Tears rolled down my cheek as I watched one of the videos. "I miss you," Kayla said with a smile into the camera, placed close to her face.

"I miss you too, babe," I said back to her.

"I wish you were here. I want cuddles."

"I'll see you soon, I promise."

"The cat misses you, too."

"Tell her I miss her. You should probably meow it so she understands."

Kayla laughed and said, "You're silly." There was a pause, then she said, "I love you."

In the video, I said, "I love you, too. So much." In reality, I sat there in the tremendous weight of guilt wishing to God or the Devil that I could turn back time.

But as the video ended, the next one came up automatically. I didn't recognize this one, and it was only a few seconds long. Curiously, I looked at the date.

It was from the night Kayla had died.

It was the video call she had made to me that night.

In my blacked out state, I had instinctively gone to record it, then forgot about it the next day. Curiosity ensnared me.

But beneath the curiosity there was terror – terror of what the video message might contain.

Hesitantly, I pressed play.

Kayla's voice crackled through the speaker. She sounded distraught, panicked, and horrified all at once. The only noise that was made was an unearthly, guttural, shrill scream of fear. The video only caught a glimpse of her face and a bit of the background of the Hole.

But barely discernible in the video was something extraordinary that caught my eye. It horrified me beyond anything I had ever seen before, a new level to the depths of fear that I could have only dreamed of.

On the very last frame of the video, Kayla's camera had caught the mirror behind the taps.

And in that mirror, something was visible. Not a whole person, but enough of one – an arm, up by the shoulder and bicep.

In the mirror was the reflection of a tattoo of an angel with the dates "1970-1998" underneath it.

It was my father.

Chapter 23

The world could have ended right there. I couldn't believe my eyes. Maybe the doctors were right, maybe I was having a psychotically manic episode and what I was looking at was a hallucination. It couldn't have been my father – I refused to believe it.

Precisely at that moment, he walked back into the bar. Hurriedly, I locked my screen and slipped my phone back into my pocket. I didn't know what to do. It couldn't have been him – could it?

"Well," he said as he took his seat across from me, "he said it doesn't look good."

I eyed him carefully, trying not to let my face betray my suspicions. "Yeah?" I asked almost challengingly.

"Yeah," he said with a sigh as he took a drink from his glass. "Homicides like this, they're inclined to throw the book at you. Especially if they try it as a double homicide."

What? My head exploded and my ears rang as he said that. My voice trembled with rising fury and fear as I spoke. "Double homicide?"

He gave me a slightly confused look and said, "Because of the kid she was carrying. I thought you knew about that? She was pregnant."

My heart stopped beating. My mind flashed back to the phone call I had with Kayla right before she died. She had told me the only other person she could talk to about it was Robin. I had told Izzy and Clyde to keep it to themselves, and I knew that there weren't any circumstances, even death, that would make them break that promise. Because they were good people, even when I wasn't. "How did you know about that?" I asked in a trembling voice.

He gave me a confused look again and said, "I mean, somebody told me – "

I cut him off. "There were only five people on this earth that knew about that. Tell me one of them besides me and maybe I'll believe you." The anger boiling at my core became hard to control.

"It was...." Jim began to say, then trailed off and never finished his sentence. Finally, he sighed and said quietly, "It was an accident, West."

My mouth hung open and my throat tightened as my brow furrowed with anger and shock. "It was you, wasn't it...." I whispered.

Jim sighed again, took a drink, and said, "I guess I owe you an explanation, don't I?" He looked like he was mulling it over for a moment before he spoke again. "I remember the first time I met her. It was before you did, actually. I served her that first night she came here. She was gorgeous, West. She was brilliant, too. I could always see why you liked her. But she needed a man in her life and you were just a boy. You bickered, you fought, you were immature. She would come here late at night and just tell me all of her problems. We would drink and laugh and I told her it would be okay. After a while, one thing led to another. We were seeing each other in the dark for a couple of months, maybe. Then I guess she grew a conscience because she came here one night and told me she couldn't do it anymore."

"You raped her," I said quietly with disgust.

"I didn't mean to," he defended. "I was drunk, she was drunk, I got mad and… Well, these things happen." He said it as if he had just broken a plate in the kitchen, like it was just a fact of life. "I tried to make it up to her, but she didn't want anything to do with me. But then…" he took another drink, "…then she told me she was pregnant."

"Please, don't…." I couldn't even finish my sentence. I knew what was coming.

"It wasn't yours, West. It was mine."

The absolute destruction of my spirit was completed at that point. But he kept going.

"She came in here that night to look for you," he said. "She felt bad about not being more upfront with you about her plans to jump state. So she came back here after she had left the first time. But by then, someone had already called me bitching about the fact that you closed down the bar so early, so I came here to check on things. You weren't around when I got here, but she walked in not five minutes after I did. She almost left as soon as she saw me, but she decided to be honest with me. She told me about the kid. She told me what she was gonna do with it, too. Guess she felt like it was the right thing to do, telling me that," Jim scoffed. "I tried to convince her to keep it. I wanted that child so badly, West. I told her we wouldn't have to tell anyone it was mine. It would look enough like you that nobody would ever get suspicious. But she wasn't going for it. She told me she was getting rid of it, then tried to leave so I grabbed her. Then she turned around and hit me right in the fucking face, and that's...that's when I lost it." He almost looked remorseful. "I'm sorry, West."

I didn't know what to say. There was nothing left for words to do. All that was left to do was to act.

As my father downed the rest of his whiskey, I glanced at the pistol sitting on the bar in between us. "That's a bad idea," he said. "I shoot to kill."

"Yeah?" I asked. I couldn't bite back the rage any longer. He hadn't noticed, but as he spoke I had slowly inched my foot through the rungs of his barstool. "So do I."

In a flash, I grabbed the bar for support, put one foot on the ground and ripped back with my other foot on the rung of his barstool and tipped it off balance, and as he fell to the floor I grabbed the .38. But he was surprisingly spry for his age and rolled out of the way before I could get a shot on him. Without hesitation, he tackled me as I jumped from my seat. I fell back onto the floor as the gun flew from my hand. His fist slammed into my jaw so hard I heard a crack, but I was just barely able to roll out of harm's way and jump to my feet. I threw a hook at him but it barely stopped the man as he charged me again and threw me back to the floor near the kitchen entrance. My back could have been broken for how badly it hurt.

Jim picked the gun up off the floor, checked the cylinder to make sure it was loaded, then pointed it at me. "You should have just gone to jail, West," he said almost disappointedly.

But I saw something that he didn't. Right behind the fryer in the kitchen, smoke had begun to rise. I thought back to my half assed job patching up the wiring, surrounded by exposed insulation. When he turned the fryer on after I got there, the spark that would start a fire finally happened. "And you should have fixed the fucking wiring yourself," I told him.

He shot me an intensely puzzled look then sniffed the air as the smoke crept into his nostrils. In a panic, he whipped around to look at the fryers. A fire had broken out and quickly grew in size. Hurriedly, with the gun still in his hand, he went to try and put it out. But as soon as his back was turned, I leapt to my feet and grabbed him by the shoulders and pulled him to the ground. The gun flew out of his hand and we struggled back and forth as the bar rapidly caught ablaze. He threw me into a few of the stools and I knocked my head against the metal rungs, but my hand caught the edge of the bar. As he lunged at me one more time, I grabbed the bottle of Macallan from the bar and shattered it across his head.

Finally, he went down.

Quickly, I darted toward the handgun and picked it up off the floor. The Hole was filled with fire now. In a matter of minutes, it would be impossible to escape. As I began to make a run for the door, my father called out my name. "West!" he roared.

I stopped in my tracks and turned around. Blood trickled down his face but he pulled himself up by the ledge of the bar and stood across from me, the fires raging at his back. It felt like I was looking at the devil himself.

He said, "You can't run from this, West. My blood is your blood. Everything I am – that's what you're capable of being. It doesn't matter what you do, it doesn't matter if you prove your innocence. None of it matters. In the eyes of these people, you'll always be guilty, even when you're not. You're always going to be the villain of the story."

My eyes stung from the smoke and the bright fire surrounding us. I coughed fiercely from the smoke in my lungs. I thought about what he said as the devil stood across from me, my body quickly growing weak from inhaling so much smoke. The pistol felt heavy in my hand. And for the first time, I had no doubt about what I was going to do.

"Be your own fucking villain." I raised the .38 and shot the devil in the eye.

Instantly, he was dead. His body collapsed to the floor.

My body finally gave up as the smoke overtook me. I realized I was facing the end, and I was okay with that. Even if nobody ever knew, Kayla had gotten the closest thing to justice she could get.

But as I fell to the floor in a coughing fit, I felt a pair of hands grab me beneath my arms and drag me out.

Chapter 24

I was dragged down the steps as my lungs cried out in agony, coughing violently until there was no more smoke in my lungs. As my savior laid me down in the street, I heard a familiar voice. "I swear to fucking god if you die on me…"

It was Clyde.

As I finally stopped coughing, he pulled me to my feet. "Holy shit," I said. "Where did you come from?"

Clyde turned his head and I saw Izzy standing by her car. She ran over to me and threw her arms around me. "West!" she cried with relief. "Holy fuck! I thought you were dead!"

"Not quite," I told her. I looked over at Clyde and said, "Clyde, I'm so sorry – "

"Water under the bridge, man," he said with a wave of his hand. "I'm not exactly a saint myself. Don't worry about it. Izzy told me you stopped drinking. Good on you, man. We all get a second chance eventually."

I wasn't sure what to say, so I said nothing, just nodded. As the windows of the bar exploded, we all three took several steps back and watched it burn. A familiar police cruiser showed up with its lights shining and siren blaring. Bill jumped out of the car. "What the hell happened?" he exclaimed.

"It was my father," I said. I pulled out my phone and handed it to Bill. "There's a recording of a video call Kayla made to me the night she died. Jim is in it. This should be all the evidence you need." Bill took the phone almost reluctantly.

"Jesus Christ," Clyde muttered. "You think you fucking know a guy...."

Izzy stood next to me and said, "I thought I lost you for a second, Superman."

"I didn't think you'd still call me that, Tinker Bell."

Izzy smiled wryly and said, "Always."

Bill radioed in the fire and said, "Fire department will be here soon."

We all stood there, watching it burn. There were moments in a man's life where he crossed a threshold, where something happened that would change things forever. That was one of those moments for me. As the inferno raged, a very familiar looking old woman slowly walked up the street and stood only a few feet from the burning building, watching it intently.

"Who the hell is that?" Clyde asked, then looked at me. "You know her?"

"Yeah," I said flatly, staring at her.

The old woman turned her head and looked at me for a second, then turned back to the fire. I still remembered what she had said to Kayla.

"She called me the devil."

AFTERWORD

If you've made it to this page, then you undoubtedly have a few questions. *Inspired by true events* and *based on a true story* are contentious phrases and hard marks to live up to in any work, whether it be film or fiction. So for the curious, and to avoid anybody being accused of murder, allow me to clear some things up.

Unfortunately, in the actual story, nobody died. Nobody went missing. Nobody was kneecapped, either. But I love violent stories as much as you do. I took real things that happened and wrapped them all up in a fictitious murder mystery.

As for everything that's not ultraviolent or murder-based, that all pretty much happened – including the date-rape accusations and the man posing as a cop calling bars. Some conversations are retold verbatim to real life. Circumstances, such as settings, order of events, relationships between people, etc., were frequently changed in order to create a cohesive narrative, but the vast majority of events and conversations not directly related to murder or Kayla's disappearance did actually happen, in one way or another. There was never a fight at a funeral, but an incredibly similar fight happened at a bar, for example. I didn't work at the bar where most of this happened, but I did work at *a* bar and it was just a more enjoyable and focused story to combine the two places into one. My father never killed anybody (that I know of), for example, but the majority of the conversations and stories between Jim and West reflect actual interactions between my actual father and myself. Also, my mother is currently very much alive, thankfully. The metaphor of the shadow just worked better without the "divine feminine," so to speak, so it felt narratively more fitting to leave a mother figure out of the story.

Heartbreak is a horrible thing – especially when you're the villain in the story. Alcoholism is a devil itself. My hope was for the missing/murder plot to act as a metaphor for the demise of my own relationship, and I hope it succeeded in being both impactful and enjoyable. If it didn't, then fuck me I guess.

No character in this story is a 1:1 analogue of any real person. These are fictional characters, even if they share dialogue with people who actually exist. That rule actually applies to damn near any story you'll ever read; all writing is autobiographical to some extent.

I haven't taken a measurement, but for those curious, I'd say this story is anywhere from 70% to 80% true – again, that's a ballpark estimate. It could be lower than that, or it could be higher.

What I will end on is this: that old woman did exist in real life, God rest her soul.

And yes…

She really called me the devil.

~ Lucas

Note from the author:

Currently, my work is only self-published through Amazon. Like any sane, rational human being, I would love for that to not be the case. Should anybody who works in publishing read this, and think it's competent enough for an actual publishing house, please, for the love of god, don't hesitate to shoot me an email.

Thanks,
Lucas D. James

lucasdjames23@gmail.com